Advance Blurbs

"*The Genizah* reconfirms that Wayne Karlin is one of my favorite novelists ever. The way he uses language to open the door to the hidden darkness of the past and shed light for our way forward is admirable. Heartbreaking, powerful, poetic, and innovative, this novel deserves its place on every bookshelf." — Nguyễn Phan Quế Mai, best-selling author of *The Mountains Sing* and *Dust Child*

"*The Genizah* is a stunner of a novel, a brilliant re-imagining of the author's own family history. In asking, *what if my parents had not left Europe?* Karlin conjures an alternative course, shining shimmering light on loves and losses and commemorating those who did not escape the Holocaust, many within his extended family. Gorgeously written and one of the most powerful, poetic books I have read, I am in awe of this novel." — Jennifer Rosner, author of *Once We Were Home*, *The Yellow Bird Sings*

"*The Genizah* is Wayne Karlin's fiction at its best. This is a painful story, uplifted and illuminated by language. It could be folklore or legend with rituals and religious intricacies; and through these we know the Jewish heart's courage and plight. A friend once said: *say it clearly and make it beautiful.* Wayne Karlin has done this in a book that will be called his masterwork." — Grace Cavalieri, Maryland Poet Laureate, Playwright

"Wayne Karlin's *The Genizah* is a work of profound empathic imagination. What might have been the fate of his parents if they had not been able to escape from the Polish town of Kolno, where most of their family were murdered by the Nazis? This brave, eloquent, and redemptive novel sears and heals, all at once." — Joyce Kornblatt, author of *Mother Tongue, The Reason for Wings,* and more

"Wayne Karlin's *The Genizah* transfigures two of literature's most venerable elements: *imagination* and *empathy*. It is a brave, beautiful, heart-deep, heartbreaking and ultimately overpowering book—necessary, and, in this strange, awful historical moment, timely." — Richard Bausch, author of *Playhouse*, editor of *The Norton Anthology of Short Fiction*

“The word “Powerful” is too tame to describe this novel of a Jewish community in Poland on the brink of the Holocaust. Scenes of mystical lyricism are interspersed with ones of intense suffering, loss, and grief. In one sense, this is the story of Jewish torment through the ages; but, even more, it is the story of particular persons in whose lives we can see something of our own. In the end, we come to realize that only one distinction should matter: whether we participate in the murder or persecution of vulnerable others, seek to protect them, or stand by while it happens.” — Michael Kinnamon, former General Secretary for the National Council of the Churches of Christ USA and author of *Summer of Love and Evil*

“This elegiac novel pays heartfelt tribute not only to Karlin’s own family but to all Holocaust victims so their stories will not be forgotten.” — Dr. Nora Gold, author of *In Sickness and In Health/Yom Kippur in a Gym,* and Editor of *Jewish Fiction .net*

THE GENIZAH

A Novel

by Wayne Karlin

 Published by Publerati.

Different versions of *Stones*, *The Smuggler's Daughter, Golem, Horses, Flow, Altar,* and *Strength,* appeared in *Rumors and Stone: A Journey,* Curbstone Press/Northwest University Press, 1995. An earlier version of "The Genizah" appeared in *The Delmarva Review,* Volume 5, 2012; and a different version of *The Boxer*, titled *The Robe,* appeared in *The Antietam Review. The Café of the Question Mark* appeared in Jewish Fiction.net, Issue 32, December, 2022.
Quoted descriptions of the Kolno massacre were taken from *The Kolno Memorial Book,* Yad VaShem Holocaust Memorial, 1971, Jerusalem, Israel and lists of family names are from *The Central Database of Holocaust Victims' Names,* Yad VaShem, Jerusalem, Israel
Trade Paperback ISBN: 979-8-9866178-2-4
Ebook ISBN: 979-8-9866178-3-1

THE GENIZAH

A Novel

by Wayne Karlin

"In each generation, each person is obligated to see himself or herself [*lirot et atzmo*] as though he or she personally came forth from Egypt."

The Passover Haggadah

"Stories can save us."

Tim O'Brien

For Ohnmar, always.

Dedicated to the victims, survivors, and descendants of the Kolno and Jedwabne massacres.

Table of Contents

Part One: The Genizah

The Genizah

Near dawn, I came across three elderly Hasids sitting on a bench filigreed with initials, hearts, and crosses. Standing near a caged, scraggly sapling on the other side of the street were seven equally ancient Chinese men. The three Jews rose in unison from their perch and began to pray, their bodies ticking back and forth like black metronomes. At the same moment, the Chinese started to conjure tai chi patterns, the movements of their hands and feet weaving slowly, as if the air had thickened to the consistency of water, a counterpoint to the frantic bobbing of the Jews. At that moment, as if called by this strange *minyan*, the sun rose.

When I turned the corner onto Henry Street, the light strengthened and I stood and watched the street transform as if the old men's dance had awakened not just the day, but a past that had been contained as fossilized seeds in the objects of the present. Burly men wearing black gabardine and screaming prices in Yiddish suddenly materialized in front of stalls overflowing with vegetables. What yesterday was a bodega was now a kosher butcher shop, the soft Latin letters of the Spanish on the window barbed into Hebrew, a black-bearded butcher scrapping together the blades of carving knives. The sprayed graffiti had unraveled from the walls and the ravaged hull of a burned-out car had dissolved into a horse-drawn cart. Old-clothes men poured out of a doorway, singing their wares. The same doorway birthed a ragged mob of children wearing yarmulkes or floppy, brimmed hats; they ran into the street and immediately began playing stick-ball games; though "began," I thought, was the wrong word: they configured into what seemed a game they had already been playing for hours or years.

I stopped and tried to immerse into the fantasy. From here, once, I probably could have seen the Towers; their absence aided the illusion being created, or re-created, though I imagined it could simply be done through camera angles. I had forgotten the filming was to begin today, even though the production company had posted notices all week. The movie was one of a recent spate of independent films about the lives of the ultra-orthodox in which a Hasid, sometimes male but more often a woman, was seduced and/or liberated from the sustaining close-knit culture and/or suffocating repression of the tradition. I let myself see the technicians dragging cameras and klieg lights out from a door on the other side of the building and a row of white trucks. A man with a bullhorn yelled at the extras. In the alley, two women were draping other extras in black, Hasidic caftans, clapping fur-rimmed *streimels* on their heads, attaching false *payot,* sidelocks. I walked past the crew and up the steps to the abandoned yeshiva that the couple with whom I was staying had converted to an art studio. The word "converted" was exactly right. *Le mot juste.* But that French phrase itself suddenly seemed nonsensical; the faith in transformative language it called for, a religion that once had wrapped me, now as remote from my heart as the morning prayers of the Hasids.

It no longer sustains, I had said to Avner and Rae when they asked me if I was writing anything new, working on a new book. I was here at their invitation, though I suspected they had offered it out of politeness and had been surprised and somewhat disturbed that I had immediately accepted. I understood their offer to be a gesture. But I had needed to get away and their own odd but lasting relationship, as well as the strange place they were playing it out, had seemed to offer a kind of refuge: Avner, an Israeli sculptor I'd once profiled for the *Herald Tribune,* had been a member of Peace Now who left the country rather than serve in the occupied territories; Rae, a one-time bond trader, the daughter of a Presbyterian army chaplain, was now a conceptual artist. What they had lost, what no longer sustained them, had drawn them together and now had drawn me into their orbit as well, in the way, I wanted to think, that exiles find each other and coalesce into their own nation.

It was the way I had thought of my wife, our marriage. I had met O when I was working in Israel; she was an ambassador's daughter from an Asian country working on her Masters in Psychology, her family privileged, as her life would have been if she had gone back home. Privileged and circumspect and mapped out. She was drawn to the security, the beauty and familiarity of her culture; she hated its rigidity, its corrupt luxuries and odious oppressions more. We were initially attracted by both the differences and the similarities in our backgrounds, a gathered nation of exiles as much as Avner and Rae, our beginning marked by wonderfully clandestine meetings in the dim, smoky cafés of Jerusalem and Belgrade, those wonderfully conspiratorial cities; until, if I want to keep up this analogy, we established borders and a flag and moved from the time of fire at dawn to the time of children and the soft risks of gardens, our attention turned to security and the national debt, all the risks of the founding years evolved into nostalgic anecdotes. We were a country, as any long marriage is; when I lost her, I lost the only other person who could truly, ever, know that country's history.

I suddenly realized that the man with the bullhorn was yelling at me through the instrument, like the voice of God. I was an intrusion in the scene, the wrong word. *Le mot unjuste.*

I opened the iron door to the yeshiva with three keys, following a ritual of locks I'd had to learn like my own morning prayer. When I first arrived here a few days ago, Avner had prepared a large bowl of rough-textured hummus, heated pita in the yeshiva's old iron stove, and let the smells of hot bread, lemon, and sesame oil drive back the musty emptiness of the building. We stuffed ourselves and got drunk on Arak, and then sang songs from Avner's childhood, the guttural tones of the Hebrew edged with an ironic and bitter tone of loss that frightened Rae. *I march with a song in my heart and a tree in my hand. We've come to build and to be built.* Avner spun prayers into senseless parodies. *If I forget thee, O Jerusalem, may my right hand lose its condominium.*

The air inside was cool and smelled of damp stone and mold and a faint, stale, miasma of rot that seemed to have permeated the walls. The walls on both sides of the cavernous entrance hall were crusted with broken-handled cups, ashy bottles, articles and photos torn jagged from newspapers, the dead, cracked eye of a television screen, velour pillows with their stuffing foaming from gashes, a greasy mattress hung like the skin of an animal. Bricolage. The exact word. Rae believed that each viewer of her art should create his own meaning, or lack thereof, from the chaotic elements she had fastened to the walls. I had never been able to think of what she did as art. The concept reminded me of a photographer who once told me—he was quoting someone else, I don't remember whom—that the best photographs were those in which the photographer didn't try to frame a portion of reality in the viewfinder. Any consciousness eroded the authenticity of the picture. Made it a lie. Why bother to take photographs at all? I had asked the photographer. Art imposed control. I had once believed that also.

In fact, a photograph I had taken, apparently scissored from a magazine and pasted into the bricolage by Rae, struck me at eye level as I walked past the wall. A girl, hysterical, carried on a stretcher by two Israeli soldiers. I usually did not use my own photographs with articles I wrote, but I didn't have a staff photographer with me that day. Three Palestinian guerillas had seized a classroom full of students at a Northern Galilee high school. When the IDF snipers had tried to take out the Arabs, they'd killed one, but only wounded the other two, who immediately set off the explosives they had wired around the classroom and turned their AK-47s on the hostages. I had rushed forward with the other reporters, past a line of wailing parents, had seen the wounded and dead children carried out of the school house door, as if in some obscene graduation straight to death.

I had seen worse. I'd seen worse in Vietnam. In fact, I had seen worse in Gaza, in an apartment building destroyed by Israeli bombs: the Israel-Palestine conflict always ready to provide crude examples of the symmetry of hate if not a symmetry of power. But this one stayed. As if the deaths were more personal, tied to me by blood. The accidental linkage of blood, in all senses of that word. That *mot juste*. I had seen worse. I had seen worse as I watched my wife of over forty years fade, her known features formed in my conscience over those years, girl to woman, reversed, blurring and bleaching to non-existence, only to re-form to me now in the face of the terrified girl in my photograph. That was what was truly linked now, no matter where I turned. The true bricolage. Creation from a seemingly diverse range of available things that somehow connected. My lost wife to that girl on the stretcher, carried as it were, out and away from the schoolhouse door. I had written about the killing in Galilee as I always did, as if putting it into print, as if the fenced tension of letters and words would render it contained and prevented. As if the pain of the girl I had framed and captured in my viewfinder and in my article had been safely dissipated into history by the art of my witness. It had not worked out. Nothing had been averted. I had come to wonder if the words I wrote about that massacre in Galilee, about all the murders I had witnessed and tried to couch into precise words, only gave license to the acts they described. Only caused them to come into my own life, the life of my wife, like a curse I had inadvertently spoken and so allowed into the world. My wife had thought so. I could see it in her accusing eyes, though whatever words she would have said were dammed in by the ventilator tube.

I knew where this was taking me and then it did and in an instance the grief expanded so quickly and fully that the inside of my skin and my skull felt like the stretched surface of a balloon on the verge of bursting. The sense of loss felt like something trying to claw its way out of my heart and guts. I closed my eyes against it, tightly, held my breath to clamp it down. Who was I now? I had been with my wife for forty-two years, the last three as a caretaker; the close-knit intimacy of that situation dissolving any sense of separation that might have still existed between us. Cut off from that structure, I was as naked as undefined as a new-born but with no desire or energy at my age to reinvent myself.

Reinvention. The word brought my mind back to the street outside, being reinvented into some movie vision of the past, Henry Street, this street where I had chosen to come this morning, had in fact been where both my mother and father, separately, had come as youngsters from Poland. To reinvent themselves. The promise of the Promised Land. My father had arrived in America as a small child; later he became a boxer, one of the crop of young, tough East Side Jews who had dominated that sport for a time. To the shock and disapproval of her brothers, my mother had declared herself independent in the new world and moved out on her own, supported herself by designing hats, and later defying the family's disapproval even further by falling in love with and marrying my father, the ex-boxer who, when they met, was already married. After my mother's death a few years ago—cancer took my father when I was five—I published a collection of stories called *Rumors and Stones,* their details imagined from her ever-changing, ever evolving anecdotes about her youth in Poland and her relationship with my father. I had written to keep something of them with me in the world and it came to me that perhaps I had come here in my grief to shine my wife's own immigrant strength, her courage to cross borders and redefine herself, her courage to love, into their story. But it all felt like a bricolage now, all discarded, disconnected pieces with no center to them. It needed to be pinned together by love, but all that hung on the wall was the chaos of loss.

A tapping noise broke into my thoughts. When I opened my eyes, I saw Rae up on a ladder, hitting a blank area of the wall lightly with a ball peen hammer, like a sculptor trying to find the secret shape within the stones. The building, she insisted, was honeycombed with secret hollows. Its acoustics were strange. Echoes within echoes.

"Any luck?" I asked her, my own voice strange in my ears.

"It still eludes me. What's happening outside?"

"Ethnic cleansing."

She laughed, more than the joke deserved. More laughter, as if an echo of hers, boomed through the black-painted door that led to the rest of the yeshiva. She glanced away, her face reddening, and I registered again the way my friends seemed to need to hide or excuse their laughter to me. Since I came, she and Avner had been treating me like a brimmed glass of water they were carrying up a steep, slippery flight of steps. Neither would utter my wife's name.

Nor could I. I felt the weight of my own presence. Rae put her hand up to her mouth, as if to stuff the escaped laughter back inside. I touched her shoulder, to say it was OK. She shook her head vigorously, as if refusing the comfort of the gesture.

I heard voices from the other room.

"Avner's cousin is visiting again," Rae said.

"He's a strange boy."

She smiled. "Lionel is my own strange, sick child."

My friends had obtained use of this building from NYU with the stipulation they would run an art program for neighborhood kids. Yesterday I'd watched Rae working with her students: Chinese, Vietnamese, African-American, and Latino kids from the Lower East Side. They stared silently at her pantomimed instructions and then compulsively stacked and restacked the materials she'd given them as if they were filling piece work quotas in a sweat shop. *Strange sick children*, I thought, but what had brought those words, *mots unjuste*, into my mind, were the eyes of the kids in the children's cancer ward I would pass on my way to see my wife in ICU. Eyes that always seemed old with a precocious, unwanted wisdom. Sometimes I would see those shorn children flocking and unflocking in fervent, silent play in their wheelchairs, the intravenous bags hooked on the metal poles above them like the strange, bulbous flags of another nation whose border I couldn't cross. The same flag that hung over my wife's bed. I tried to smile at Rae now, a grotesque gesture of reassurance, but she shuddered and in that moment, in that tremble, I saw, as if through the coaching frame of a viewfinder, the empty dimensions of this building abandoned of its true purpose, her bricolage tacked to its hollow walls like the exploded elements of an abandoned planet.

I walked into the next room. Avner was brewing Turkish coffee on a small gas stove. He smiled at me and bobbed his head in swift nods, as if it was the blade of an axe. Next to him, his American cousin, Lionel, a short, thin boy in a white shirt and black trousers, a knit yarmulke on his head, glanced at him and then bobbed his head also, cueing on Avner's motion as if it were the custom of a religion he wanted to learn.

"Shalom, Avi," he called to me. He liked using the diminutive of my given Hebrew name, Avram.

Avner rolled his eyes. "Do you know what shalom means, Lionel? Shalom means war."

"Shah," Lionel said. He waved his hand around the room, as if someone would hear.

Avner grinned. "Did you know that Lionel once studied here?"

I stared at the boy. "Is that true?"

"Until I was thirteen, I danced with the Hasids. For Avner's sins."

Avner clapped his cousin's shoulder. "He chides me for leaving the holy land for the fleshpots. For becoming at last the rootless cosmopolitan I've always dreamed of becoming." He began to agitate the coffee that had started to bubble thickly in the small brass *finjon.*

"Why did you leave," I asked Lionel.

The boy didn't answer, only helplessly waved his hand around the room again.

I suddenly heard a sharp cry from the other room. Rae was still on top of the ladder. As the three of us rushed in, she raised a finger to her lips, and then gripped the hammer and tapped it against the wall. The small blow set off a hollow, tocking echo. She pounded faster against the skin of the wall, her hand trembling with excitement or fatigue.

"Hang on," Avner said. He left the room again, came back with a short-handled sledge hammer. He started to hand it up to Rae, but I put a hand on his forearm, looked up at Rae. "May I?"

"I can do it."

"Please." She looked down at me, her eyes widening, and I heard, as if an echo, what she must have heard in my voice. "Sure, no problem," she said finally, and came down.

I climbed the shaky, aluminum tripod. The place she had been tapping was scarred with half-crescent wounds. I struck the center of the same area, tentatively at first, but then hard and then harder. I could feel the reverberating thud of each blow in my bones. The plaster started to fall off in ragged chunks, exposing the brick wall underneath, red as a wound.

I concentrated on one brick, hitting it along its edges. Finally it began to inch backwards, grating in protest. I delivered a final, sharp blow to its center and it fell through, inside the wall. There was a dull thud and a rustle, soft as a whisper. I leaned forward, put my eye to the hole. I could see only blackness. I called below for a flashlight, and Avner brought it up the ladder, crowding against my back. When I inserted it through, it blocked the hole and I could not see anything. I handed the light back to Avner and started to strike at the bricks again.

Plaster and chips of brick flew around my head, opened small shrapnel cuts on my cheeks. My arm felt more weighted with each blow. Avner put a hand on my back. But the gesture, intended to be comforting, only annoyed me. I shrugged against it, thinking Avner would ask to take over. The bricks, their center support gone, were now easier to dislodge. Within ten minutes there was a hole large enough to peer into.

I leaned over the top of the ladder, into the torn lip of the hole. A thick, fetid smell wafted into my nostrils and a gust of stale cold air chilled the sweat on my skin. I flicked on the flashlight and had to stifle a scream. Revealed by the probing beam were thousands of Hebrew letters, words, lying limply atop each other, like corpses or dreamers. As the light touched them, they seemed to stir, rustle. Here and there individual words stood out, like suddenly recognized faces in a crowd. As my eyes adjusted I saw the pages, yellowed, brittle; the letters and words seemed not imprinted on them but rather hovering a millimeter above them, like their breath. Scattered throughout were dark sarcophagi—books—as well as the lighter oblongs of the fallen bricks. I stared, transfixed, my head buzzing, the letters seeming to rise in a cloud around my face. I was suddenly aware of

Avner's hand, pulling at me, Rae's voice rising querulously from the base of the ladder.

"A Genizah," Lionel said, after his turn on the ladder.

"Explain, rabbi," Avner demanded.

"A tomb for books. You need to bury holy books, and even their pages that are torn or smeared, in a consecrated place. You're not allowed to destroy them. They contain the Holy Name. The loose pages are called *Shemot,* names."

"We should tell someone," Rae said uneasily. "Shouldn't we?"

"We should brick it up again," Avner said.

"Yes," Lionel said. "They would want that."

"Who?"

He didn't answer. "But only if it's done properly."

"Properly?"

"A proper funeral. Now that we've opened it, it's desecrated. There has to be another proper burial."

Avner grinned. "Is that right, Rabbi Hashish? Or are you making it up as you go along?"

I climbed the ladder again and reached into the hole, touching the paper delicately, as if it would cringe away from me. My forefinger and thumb grasped the spine of a book.

"I want to see what's here first," I said.

"No," Rae said.

"Yes," I said. I didn't recognize my own voice. Rae looked at me and shuddered, then nodded slowly. I knew I was using my loss and grief to bully them, but I didn't care; I needed to touch what was inside the wall, bring it into the light.

After my wife was gone, I had constructed a room from memory. It was a room near water. The yellow sunlight gauzed through the flimsy curtains was the filtered light of memory. I put myself back in that room and put my wife back in it and lived there in a loop played over and over, paused, re-wound, played; if I stopped it would burn, a point of flame would flare in the center of the frame from the place where our bodies were joined and expand swiftly in a fiery circle that I felt in my stomach and chest like the burn of grief. In that room we didn't need words.

The chamber was a kind of bee-honeycomb cell hollowed into the otherwise solid brick interior of the wall separating the smaller room from the entrance hall. It had been made, probably, Avner maintained, as the building was being constructed. He sat at the base of the ladder, staring at the black hole, theorizing, concentrating on the construction, but refusing to speculate about or even touch the books and pages I was pulling from the Genizah, handing them down to Lionel, who reverently arranged them in neat piles on one of Rae's tarps, all the while muttering prayers. Rae sat next to him, rocking as if at prayer herself.

It took most of the day to empty the hidden chamber, scooping the loose pages out carefully and handing them down, gripping the books delicately; some of them falling to pieces anyway, as if released by that human touch. When the first quarter of the floor inside had been cleared, I wriggled into the hole.

My body cut off most of the light from outside. I had the flashlight, but I didn't turn it on. The air was thick with dust and smelled of mold. I closed my eyes and felt the words like small stirrings against my skin. I drew my knees up to my chin and sat perfectly still. As still as an unopened book. I remembered reading a story in which being dead was described as being a book on a shelf. You stayed dead until and unless someone took you off the shelf and opened you. What if no one ever opened you? All the books unread, buried and bricked in, unmourned. I picked up a handful of pages and pressed them to my face.

*****

That night, we didn't sleep. We lit kerosene lanterns and passed around the tattered prayer books, Talmudic interpretations, coda, commentaries. The Hebrew, Avner said, was archaic. We sat on the stone floor, our shoulders touching, and with Lionel leading and Avner translating, chanted passages to each other. *And Rabbi Meir's wife Beruiah said, did you not tell me we must return to the Owner that which He entrusted to our care?* Later, the four of us formed a circle and danced a wild, uncoordinated hora as if at last succeeding at what the movie being filmed outside had attempted: raising the ghosts of the black-clad, white brillo-bearded rabbis and yeshiva *bochurs* who would gather in the hall on Simhat Torah, dance, sing, pound their fists on the long study tables in ecstatic throes of joy, their lank sidecurls sticking to pale faces gleaming with sweat and joyful certainty. Lit by a kerosene lantern that burned with a blue, unearthly light, the room came alive with gigantic and fluid shadows. At dawn, the sun began to stream in through the smudged windows atop the front door and suddenly incandescent dust motes swirled in the air.

Later, Avner drove his pickup to a masonry he used sometimes for sculpting supplies, and came back with another ladder, a bag of cement mix, more bricks, and plaster. After we made the preparations, we took turns using the shower in the basement, and then dressed in clean clothes; we men in white shirts with black trousers—I needed to borrow a pair from Avner—and Rae in a long Arab dress with embroidery on the front, a scarf draped over her head. Avner had also brought back—or had among his own materials, I was not sure—two long wooden boxes, which he had painted black. We arranged the papers and books inside the boxes; we would place them inside the hole, seal them again. Lionel chanted the mourner's prayer: *yisgadal v'yishadash sh'me rabbo, b'olmo deevro chirush.* Avner touched my shoulder, as he had on the ladder, and let his sculptor's hand, whitened with plaster dust, rest there, a holding weight. *Weep for the mourners, not for the departed,* Lionel sang. Avner placed the two ladders against the wall, one on either side of the hole. He and I bent over to pick up a box; we carried it up between us. As I placed the box inside the opening, a pulse leapt in my hand and I felt a flutter of hard, miniscule wings inside my veins. Behind a sudden veil of tears, I could see the letters rising and dancing like Hasids, like a story that was coming to life to keep the world from flying to pieces.

Interlude: Our Voice

Our Voice

Words scattered from the Genizah like a panicked cloud of black birds, spread a net against the sky, wove strands of nothing, as if a web of faint breaths. If words call the world, can they re-form the world as well? The light inside the Genizah flickers, elongates like a candle flame caught in an uncertain wind, dances shadows against the curved wall. On the floor, one book remains. A single gilted word forms onto its black cover: קולנו. The Hebrew letters dance into place, one by one, simultaneously flicking into English letters: Kolno. My mother's town in Poland. I see a folded sheet of paper sticking out from the pages of the book.

In the cold caverns of Ellis Island in which my mother, my grandmother, and my uncle waited to be renamed, the ceilings, stained with fantastic shapes by the drifting dreams wafted up from the immigrants' cots, pressed down on my mother's forehead like the walls inside the hollow of the Genizah. The shapes in the ceiling guttered and changed as the shadows of the people below played against them, like the flickers of a film she had once seen projected against a sheet hung on the wall of the heder in Kolno. In the film a bride had been possessed by a dybbuk: could such malevolent spirits follow them here? Pass as shadows through a dybbuk-Ellis Island, the American inspectors re-naming them: what names would they give demons who took over minds and souls? Perhaps, instead, as they changed the name each person brought before them, the inspectors were inserting American dybbuks, seizing and discarding their old souls like the heaps of clothing she had seen piled in a room they passed.

Through the narrow bars of the window, as the sun sets, she can see the Lady holding her torch high; was she beckoning or barring? Her face changed as the light changed.

I take the sheet of paper from the book and unfold it. A list. I have seen it before. The name of the authority that issued it blurs as I try to read it, the ways words in a dream are blurred or elusive. But the details in the list can be seen clearly: Our family name, first name, town, country, fate: **Brikman, Avraham, Kolno, Poland, Murdered/ Brikman, Gittel, Kolno, Poland, Murdered.** Twenty-three names; I know the number without counting, although I am not certain of the relationship. Twenty-three left behind.

Kolno, they whisper from the ditch where their bones lie, still entangled. Their voices. Our voice. The word voice in Hebrew is "Kol." "Kolno, Kolaynu," my mother would sing, a dimly remembered ditty from her girlhood that Judaized the Polish name to mean "Our Voice." Before the war, most of the town had been Jewish, a shetl, Yiddish its first language, and Jews not allowed in the Polish school: my mother had studied Hebrew in a Beit Yakov, a school for Jewish girls. I count the names, touching each one as I do. Twenty-six. I count again. Three extra names have been tagged at the end of the list. **Brikman, Sarah Gittel, Kolno, Murdered/Brikman, Yitzhak, Kolno, Poland, Murdered/Brikman, Raḥel, Kolno, Poland, Murdered.** My grandmother, my uncle, my mother, all of whom had left that place, found sanctuary in America. The three lines appear as I touch them, fade to white when I lift my finger. Appear, disappear. Then a fourth line, at first blurry, but sharpening into clarity: **Karlinsky, Elazar, Kolno, Poland, Murdered**. My father. Who had never been there.

A part of me knows I am creating the dream even as it forms. A lucid dream. But why this dream, why add those names to the fallen? Stories can save us, a friend of mine had written. But why this story? I knew their real stories. In the Lower

East Side, near the yeshiva where words had been entombed in a Genizah, my mother, daughter of Pinhas and Sarah Gittel, had escaped from Europe and then burst herself out of the clinging web of family and into the new world, and my father, descendent of a rabbinical dynasty, had fled that world and shaped himself into a street fighter and a boxer. Later, he had married an older woman who owned a millinery manufacturing business; she had become obsessed with him. She picked him like she had chosen a prime brisket from a butcher shop and then she sliced him up, my mother always claimed; their relationship, she insisted, was unhealthy and strained, and when she came to work for him, they had fallen in love. He had divorced his wife, but the status of the divorce was contested and he and my mother had gone to Mexico to be married.

Once, I had written the stories my mother told me about her life in Kolno as a weave of dreams, a game of rumors, where a secret is passed down a line of children, whispered from one set of lips to an ear and so on, so that as it travels it is changed, taking on the truth of each child through whom it passes. So at the end it is the same but changed. Reinvented, even as America had allowed my mother and our family not just to live but to reinvent themselves, which is the process of living. I had written how my grandmother Sarah Gittel had been halfway across the Atlantic on her way to America, when she removed her Orthodox wig and threw it in the ocean. Then she shook her head rapidly, as if waking the crown of real hair she'd allowed to grow secretly under the wig. The hairs on the wig wriggled like the tentacles of a sea creature as it floated on the surface, until it soaked in the weight of the water and sank. She watched the disappearing black dot of the hairpiece with a smile that shocked her children, my mother, and uncle, as much as the action they'd just witnessed. It was a stranger's smile. It threw into doubt the whole country of memory.

Sarah Gittel's brother Tzvi Haim Lobel and his wife, Miriam Beila, along with thirty-three others of the extended Lobel family were murdered in Kolno in 1941; her other brother Avraham, after whom I received my Hebrew name "Avram," his wife Gittel Tovah, their children Zelda, Rivka, Shalom, and Pinchas, were murdered near Kolno, in the town of Jedwabne, where many of the Jewish victims had been locked into a barn by Polish collaborators and burned to death.

If Avraham and Gittel Tovah's daughter Bruria, a Zionist at sixteen, hadn't defied her parents and smuggled herself to Palestine in 1936, if her other brothers Haim,

Moshe, and Zelig hadn't fled to Argentina a year earlier; if Tzvi and Miriam Beila's three sons Dov, Yitzhak, and Avraham, hadn't fled into the forest and become partisans; if they hadn't been tough enough, or smart enough, or simply lucky enough; if my grandmother, and mother, and her brothers and sisters and my father and his family, had not torn themselves away from a place they and their ancestors had lived for hundreds of years, in a town and on a continent where they had always been unwelcome guests, this would have been their fate.

What if Sarah Gittel and my parents had stayed in Europe, to end as lines in a list of murders? If their story had been one not of escapes but of capture; if they'd been woven into the murder they'd only escaped because some in their families had the guts and the luck to twist out of a trap. I knew little of my father's family there; his death, when I was five, had severed me from whatever their stories might have been. But I knew what the end of my mother's story would be if she had stayed in Poland. It had been foreshadowed in the blood that had awakened in helpless echo from her body, her first menstruation that occurred when she had seen the blood of the murdered flowing in the gutters before her house during the pogroms that had rolled through Kolno like harbingers of the greater massacres that would happen in

1941. I knew about the massacres in the market square, the mock burial of the statue of Lenin that became a pogrom, the ditch of the murdered from which we'd been spared, escaped, but that inevitably extended in my mind to the ditch at My Lai, in the war to which I had gone. I knew the raw pain of loss which was the same for one person torn away or for two thousand, the loss that must be held up into the light to find how it can speak to love.

At the Passover table we are admonished not to tell the story of anguish and slavery and liberation as if it happened to those old Jews, but as if it is happening to us, as if we are there with them, of them, the whips on our backs, the bitterness and the sweetness in our mouths. To remind us, as grief reminded us, of what needed to be saved, of what needed to be suffered in order to be saved.

What if they had never left?

The wig flings itself out of the ocean and nestles back on Sarah Gittel's head. The ship flies in reverse through the ocean, the spray from its wake arcing down to the water it churns through; she and Raḥel and Yitzhak vomited back into Europe, dust flying from wheels and hooves as they are drawn, yanked, back to Kolno, to my grandfather's grave, the stones they had placed on his headstone flying back into their hands, flung back on the earth. Their earth, with their father, their husband nested in it; why should they leave, demands Sarah Gittel, go to a land of cannibals? They are pulled back to the market square, the river Lavnes boiling black over white rocks that stand like the tombstones that mark the path of life as it veers uncontrollably into oblivion.

Part Two: If We Had Stayed

"In the three actions that occurred from the beginning of July 1941 to the beginning of August, all the other Jews of Kolno, over two thousand people, were murdered. Halina Golshovska-Glaser, one of the Kolno Poles who had been horrified by the events in her town, wrote to a Jewish friend:

Dear friend, no ghetto was established in Kolno. The town was too small so the Germans murdered all the Jews in a very short time. When they had collected them all in the marketplace, they loaded their luggage onto special lorries: the men in one group, the women and children in another, and were sent in two directions—to Meschtshevoye and to the other side of Zabiele, where the antitank trenches and special ditches had been dug. The Jews were ordered to undress and were machine-gunned. All of them—those who fell dead together with the wounded and unhurt—were heaped into the trenches. People who witnessed all this can tell that for three days the earth there was seen to quiver and tremble."

— *The Kolno Memorial Book*

Chapter One: Stones

Whenever she sees Elazar, a broken-nosed ex-boxer, now a horse trader and smuggler, walking through the market square, reaching to buy a fruit or flowers, even walking with his intended Rivka Mendl, Raḥel closes her eyes and sees him in the river, naked and shining, as he'd looked when she had gone with the other girls, giggling, squealing, pushing each other, to spy on the boys when they went to bathe. Tit for tat; they knew the boys had done the same on the bath day for girls and women, peeking in between slats in the bathhouse. She did not giggle, squeal, or push. She saw him rising from the river draped with mist, as if born only for her. It was true. *HaShem* had made a mistake. She would have him.

For weeks now, they had been meeting at that same river. Taking walks, to pick mushrooms or berries, talking. He had opened to her how he felt a stranger in the town, a stranger all his life, among both Poles and Jews. A stranger, he finally confided to her, to Rivka Mendl, the woman he was pledged to marry. Raḥel had told him of her father's death, the plans to emigrate that never came true. Of her brothers, of the tensions between herself and her mother, of her desire to leave, to leave, to leave. She wished she were bold enough to tell him what she had seen, to ask him to bathe with her. The idea sent a shiver through her blood; she held her tongue, feared he would see her as a *kurveh*, a whore. He had been a disappointment, he told her, to his father, Herschel, a learned man, a *melamed* in the cheder to whom many of the poorer Kolno Jews would come with religious questions because of his knowledge of Torah and Talmud. Even some Poles would consult him, with weighty domestic or business or even spiritual problems. They trusted his wisdom and his beard.

She loved that he had been a disappointment to his father. To her mother, Sarah Gittel, Raḥel had been a stone. Sarah Gittel had given birth to thirteen children, but six died during or immediately after birth or from illness. Except for her son Dov, she treated the survivors with suspicious irritation. Whenever she looked at them, a cold, transparent carapace formed over her eyes, like something sliding up from her heart. After the stillborn birth of her third child, she'd seized the small corpse from Maja, the Polish midwife, and began kissing and panting over the child's icy flesh, rubbing its limbs between her hands. Maja had to tear the corpse away from her as she had torn the child from the grip of Sarah Gittel's body. When the fourth child was also stillborn, Sarah Gittel tried to bite into her own wrists, smiling up at Maja, holding her own white arm like a bone. Cold, she said, and bared her teeth. Maja saw Sarah Gittel's soul turn into a fluttering bird trying to escape from her eyes. Instructing her sister Maja to hold her down, she went outside and found a stone, heated it on the stove, wrapped it in swaddling and brought it to Sarah Gittel. She allowed Sarah Gittel to hold the solid form and feel its heat through the cloth, then snatched it away. You see, she said, your baby is alive. At that instant Maja saw an image of her own hands molding lumps of bloody flesh to life and the notion came to her that she could stroke the stone to existence, knead its heat to flesh, a thought of such terrible arrogance she knew it must have been put into her mind by the dybbuk that had entered Sarah Gittel at the moment of her body's openness; she had seen it happen before to her Jewish patients. Sarah Gittel snatched the heated stone back from Maja with a superhuman strength. She opened the cloth, laughed wildly and pressed her lips to the rock, burning them. Then she lay back against the pillows, pressing the stone to her breast, murmuring in a strange drone through the ring of new blisters on her lips.

The first child not stillborn was a girl, Bechele, who later died in the influenza pandemic. The first time Sarah Gittel nursed the infant, she felt its lips turn into a hot ring of stone around her nipple and shrieked. After that, her children, until weaned, were given over to Maja, who hired as a wet nurse.

Raḥel had spent the first five years of her life in the cramped dark house of the two sisters. She would suck at one of Maja's breasts while Maja's daughter Wanda nursed at the other, black hair next to blond hair. At night, by the fireplace, Maja would tell both girls stories from the Bible, as well as stories of the witches and demons who inhabited the forests around Kolno. On each Jewish Sabbath, Maja would tell Raḥel the story of Eve, the first woman, exiled from paradise for what Maja called the sin of wanting to name names. Then Raḥel would be washed and scrubbed with ice cold well water, dressed in the clothing Maja only took out for that day, taken to the Brikman house and presented to her mother, as if a decision were to be made. Sarah Gittel would look at her coldly, as if she was just another stone brought to fool her.

Chapter Two: Christ-Killer

Raḥel likes that Elazar is an orphan. A stone. His mother had died two years before. It didn't take his father much longer to follow his wife into the Other World. He had already torn his shirt and sprinkled ashes on his head to mourn his son as a lost soul long before that.

What else can Raḥel add to this list of answers to a question no one has asked her? She likes that he had been a fighter, a talent that had no place in his father's world or in her mother's. He'd become a boxer during his service in the Polish army. Unlike many Jewish boys, unlike her brother Dov, he had not tried to escape the army. For a time, he told her, he'd had a delusion that such service was a way to gain respect and acceptance from the Poles, not just for himself, but for all Jews. How did you get over it, that delusion, she asked. My fellow soldiers cured me, he'd replied. He'd believed Pilsudski's promises that Jews would be equal citizens in a free Poland. He'd seen Jews slaughtered by the Bolsheviks for being Jews in every town they liberated; in the same towns he'd seen Polish soldiers and peasants slaughter Jews for being Bolsheviks. Personally, he wanted to hone himself into a weapon. He told her he had been with the 14th Infantry Brigade, whatever that meant; he had fought with Pilsudski against the Bolsheviks, and was wounded in the battle of Kolno, during which she and her mother had once again hidden like mice. From both sides. She likes that his time in the army made him feel like a stranger among the Jews, that being a Jew made him feel like a stranger in the army. It is how she feels also, or tells herself she feels. She likes that he knows gangsters in Bialystok. She likes that he feels dangerous. She likes that her mother doesn't like him. She doesn't care that he is ten years her senior, and promised to a witch fifteen years or more years older than he.

A black year on her.

She has been seeing him during the self-defense drills set up for Jewish youths by the Bund, though she, they, needed to pretend there was nothing between them. Elazar is in charge of training the group. They meet Sundays in the Piska Forest, practice with sticks pretending to be rifles and real knives. The youth group itself had been organized, at first by her brother Dov, in response to the attacks against Jews. Thousands murdered in pogroms. Though after the war with the Soviets the Poles no longer called them pogroms, but simply riots. Pogrom was a Russian word. The Jews still used it.

Semantics, Elazar says, shaking his head. We're not here to blab, blab, blab. Pogrom, riot, murder, feast, famine, squawk, squawk. Keep walking. This isn't a rabbinical debate.

They have been hiking for two hours or more, carrying heavy branches on their shoulders. Branches whip her face. Her feet are killing her and there is a stitch of pain in her side.

What would you call what we're doing, Rabbi, she called out. With these ridiculous sticks. Are we going to plant them into the tochuses of the goyim who come to kill us, wait until they grow into trees to impale them?

She sees him flinch slightly at the word "Rabbi," smiles to herself.

The other hikers mutter, whisper. A girl, Chana Mendoza, giggles.

Do you think what we're doing is a joke, Miss Brikman?

She does not.

Where are you, he asks her.

In Kolno.

Where are you?

In *Gehenna.*

When I was in the army, everyone in our training company was given a nickname. Joker. Farmer. Drunkard. Pig-fucker. Do you know what my nickname was?

I think you are going to tell me.

Christ-killer. Hurry up, Christ-killer. Crawl through that mud, Christ-killer.

She laughs. And did you?

Hurry up? Crawl? Of course.

No. Did you kill any Christs?

Many.

She sees he is not returning her smile. I'm sorry, she says.

For example, he says, there was the town of Komorov. After our soldiers had gone through. I saw old men and women with their skulls crushed. I saw old women and little girls they'd raped with their stomachs ripped open. Worse, I saw babies still alive, with their fingers sliced off. Jews. That was one town. It was not the only town.

Does he think she doesn't know where she is? Why she is running through these miserable, mosquito buzzing woods carrying a stick like a fool? She is nineteen. The first time she had bled as a woman was while she was watching the blood of murdered Jews foaming through the street gutters. While she was watching the blood of the Jewish girls and women raped in the middle of the square. A different blood. Devorah Ratner who was six years old. Chava Feynsteyn who was sixty. Only the ones she had seen. Afterwards her father bricked up the street-level opening through which she had peered. Now every month when she had her flow she felt like the memory of murder was inside her body, a weight inside her belly, added to with each pogrom, with the war when the Germans came to fight the Russians, and the war after that when the Polish army, Elazar's army, had fought the Red Cavalry. A continuous rattle of gunfire had permeated the walls. Plaster and brick dust had drifted down onto their heads, coated their hair and skin. Her monthlies were blood calling to blood.

Chapter Three: Flow

She remembers how it was the first time. Jews disappeared. First it was the poor: the market-square beggars, the fixers, wood cutters, bristle makers and tanners who lived in the dank wooden hovels and tangles of dark alleys near the cemetery. Then those with more to leave behind. One day they were home, people Raḥel had known all her life, the next day they were gone, their houses empty. The shape of the world melted. One day she woke up and her brother Dov was gone to join their older brothers, Max and Herman, in America. Soon her sisters Bella and Faigl vanished also, into the Golden Land. Her little brother Yitzhak was brought home draped over the humpback of his teacher, the dwarf Gedalie Ali. In the doorway they looked like the photograph of Siamese twins she'd seen. Chang and Eng. Two legs, four arms, two heads. Her brother and Gedalie Ali were sealed together with blood. Teacher and pupil. Her mother, Sarah Gittel, screamed but then fell silent. A strange birth, she muttered, her eyes going distant, as Gedalie Ali peeled Yitzhak from his back and lay him on the horsehair couch. Yitzhak's hand was shattered and bloody, his face swollen and bruised. Blood calls to blood, Gedalie Ali said. The world's unknitting. Beware.

Maja, the Polish midwife, who had been her wet nurse, vanished from her life also, though her father told her Maja was still in Kolno, afraid to work for them. Invisible borders had trenched through the town.

Sarah Gittel refused to clean. Raḥel tried to hold the house together but the furniture was always so furry with dust it seemed to her the tables and chairs were blurring into the air. She found plates with scraps of rotting meat left to stink in the halls. A spot of green mold on the ceiling became a continent. Her father's face was stamped with worry. One moment Sarah Gittel berated him for not forcing them to flee with Dov to America, the next she cursed him for worrying her with his precautions, the cave-like space he'd dug out under the floorboards, secretly carting the dirt off to the forest during the night.

Why should we disappear into a hole—we've done nothing. What's coming for us?

He laughed bitterly. The century, he said. Raḥel joined nervously and involuntarily in his laughter; she didn't find what he said funny but she'd never heard her father laugh like that. Sarah Gittel glared at her. At that very moment, her body, for the first time, began to bleed. She felt herself flowing away. Mama, she called. She reached under her skirt, drew back red fingers. The entire house began to tremble and shift. Dust demons rose and danced before her eyes. Yitzhak moaned from his sick bed. Do you see what you did? Sarah Gittel screamed at her. Outside she heard the crack of a hundred thunderclaps and instantly an echoing crack appeared in the wall. Books fell from the shelves. Here it is now, her father muttered. She burst into tears. Her mother turned and slapped her so hard her ears rang. Now cry, *pickholtz*, simpleton. See if the goyim won't come because you weep.

A series of explosions shook the house again. Glass fell from the windows facing the market square. Between the stalls, a girl, her friend Miriam Weiss, ran by, chased by a group of laughing Poles, their faces streaked with dirt and blood, as if they'd been released from the earth. Through the windows Raḥel saw them run from one frame to the other as if passing into a series of pictures hung in her mind. Sarah Gittel pulled the curtains shut, stared at her with hatred, as if holding her responsible. Quickly, little fool, bring the food, the water; help for once, help with your brother. There's no time for your nonsense now.

In the darkness under their floor, they sat, necks bent,

among the sacks of potatoes that Pinhas had lugged down, along with Yitzhak's mattress. In his hands, he held the green ledger that contained a record of his business transactions.

We'll eat that last, Sarah Gittel said. What were you doing upstairs?

I thought you were going to bring down more of the food and blankets, Pinhas said. And the water—we only have one jug. Armies clash above our heads; who knows how long we'll have to burrow here.

Is it a wife's job to think of such things? Sarah Gittel said. Did I bury us here? She lit a candle and glanced at her daughter, a look full of blame. What's come from me? Her daughter asked Sarah Gittel when she'd drawn her into the bedroom to staunch her flow. The sin of Eve, Sarah Gittel had said, wadding linen. The Lord punished her for wanting to take his Power by giving it to her. Now you're so blessed also. Mazel Tov. Say nothing to your father.

More explosions shook the house. Dust fell from the planks above their heads, coating their flesh. Raḥel felt the floor above her head press in on her: the space was too shallow for any of them to stand up.

You've buried us before we're dead, Sarah Gittel said to her husband.

We'll be safe here.

We'll grow like potatoes with our heads in the earth.

Raḥel sat perfectly still in the semidarkness, her flesh trembling with the walls. She felt sick with power. Yitzhak cried and moaned. His head was hot as a stove. But she won't cry. She won't let any more of her body drain out and become things in the world.

A day, a night, another day, another night. They huddled in the darkness. Shrieks pierced through the thick walls; at times they heard footsteps thudding over their heads. Her father took the ax he used to chop wood and sat with it across his lap. Worse than the footsteps was the scurrying and scratching all around her. Warm hairy bodies scampered across her legs. When she started to scream, Sarah Gittel clamped a hand over her mouth, whispered in her ear. Be quiet, they're just fellow hiders in the darkness. Keep them from your brother.

Raḥel curled her body around Yitzhak's head, flailing her arms or kicking whenever the rats got close. The water was gone. In the darkness they felt themselves losing first time, then form, so every once in a while, Sarah Gittel had to light a candle to bring them back to themselves. Their lips swelled and cracked. When Rahel swallowed she felt her swollen throat constrict painfully around a thin sharp shard of dry bone. Yitzhak had stopped moaning. When she brought her face close to his in the darkness, his breath was cold and rank, the last trapped breath in the mouth of a corpse. He stared blankly. Mama, she croaked. Sarah Gittel lit a candle and looked at her son. She picked up the chamber pot and carried it to Yitzhak. Cradling his face in her lap, she filled a small cup, poured it into his cracked lips. The stench intensified in the air. The urine dribbled over his lips, down his chin. Raḥel saw his throat constricting. Sarah Gittel drank next, gestured to her daughter, her husband. It's only us, she said. The candlelight flickered against the walls. Raḥel saw in it the flame of her mother's anger, pushing out, holding the walls firm against the world.

What kind of time do potatoes know, growing with their heads in the earth? She was no longer sure how many days had passed in the world of day and night. Sometimes moans and whispers penetrated the thick walls as if they'd become thin as membrane. Wisps of smoke drifted through invisible cracks. A thick acrid stink filled the air. Her father rocked in prayer. She watched her mother looking at him with a contempt she suddenly understood. She heard shots, a series of thuds against the walls of the house, the clomp of footsteps.

Don't worry; they'll have to chop through the floor

to get to us, her father whispered.

The goyim don't have axes? Sarah Gittel asked.

Yitzhak moaned. The noise stopped. It doesn't matter, Sarah Gittel said. Soon we'll dry up and blow away like dust. She lit the candle, picked up the chamber pot, shook it tiredly so they could see it was empty, dry. They had nothing left to piss into it.

He's dying, she said. We're dying, dried and husked as if caught in webs.

Pinhas, gripping the ax, crawled across to the wall on the market square side of the house. He and Sarah Gittel stared at each other, then he turned from her gaze and began to hit the blunt end of the ax head against the plaster wall. A patch of red appeared as the plaster fell; Rahel saw the outlines of bricks that looked lighter, cleaner than the rest of the wall.

He slammed the ax against the bricks until they cracked and fell apart, then pulled out the pieces. Raḥel saw a white cataract, glowing over the hole. Her father reversed the ax and smashed the handle end against the whiteness. The ice cracked and suddenly his face is pale and thin in the moonlight and she could see the preserved world outside, held between white teeth. He reached into the opening. Sarah Gittel blew out the candle and crawled next to him. He handed her a shard of ice; she sucked it greedily. He reached cautiously outside, scooped in a handful of dripping snow. Come, Sarah Gittel whispered to Raḥel, come help me take some to your brother.

Raḥel heard a scraping noise and turned quickly. Yitzhak, his bandaged hand bleeding, his face white, had risen to his hands and knees and was staring at the glowing white sphere that her father had opened in the wall. He began pulling himself towards it over the dirt floor. Yitzhak, she whispered, get back. But Sarah Gittel smiled at him, nodded. Come, come to moisture, to light. Come, *kaddish*, her father said, come to life, come, Raḥel. Yitzhak inched towards the opening. Raḥel crawled beside him so they arrived at the hole at the same time. They wrapped their arms around each other. Entwined they peered through the blind, cracked eye. Chang and Eng. They both pushed their heads against the opening as if suckling together. They stuck their tongues out and licked at the icy liquid. They reached out and stuffed snow into their mouths. The cold lump melted slowly in Raḥel's mouth, its released moisture softening the dry, cracked membranes of her tongue, seeping coldly and deliciously down her throat, numbing her lips. She looked through the hole. Here were the cobblestones of the street, shining under a rime of ice, the market square across it held by the jagged rat teeth of ice at the top and a clean lip of snow at the bottom, nimbused in a halo as if it had just been created. She licked the snow.

As her eyes hunted, she saw the broken world born from her body. Tongues of flame licked the sky behind the market square and in the square the stall of Dulovich, the kosher butcher was burning. For an instant she thought she saw the form of the butcher himself, hanging in his stall like a side of meat. Other shapes were scattered on the ground like broken dolls.

Strange figures suddenly ran into the street, weaving and ducking in a grotesque dance. They screamed silently, smoke pouring from their nostrils, faces distorted and blackening. Purim, Yitzhak whispered, his flesh shivering against hers.

She stared. Framed by a glowing halo of whiteness, the very mouth of astonishment, the figures outside danced in the snow and fell into twisted postures and attitudes, like strange black letters written against the snow. A young man on a white horse rode by out of a miracle. He suddenly threw up his hands, clutched his breast and fell into the street, his eyes locked to hers, rolling like a horse's eyes. Yitzhak trembled with silent laughter. Blood gouted from the young man; it gushed magically through the gutter to her window, blood to blood. She reached her fingers out into the warm stream and brought them back to her lips, connected herself to the flow of the world.

Chapter Four: Curses

She can still taste it on her lips. Doesn't Elazar think she knows where she is? Before the war Kolno was in Russia, after it was in Poland, moved not as a chess piece across a board but rather as if the board had moved under the chess pieces. It doesn't matter. All Raḥel knows is she is still in the Land of the Jews. The land of Jews' benches and humiliations and mobs that come to murder and rape as inevitably as seasons. Is it any wonder she loves Elazar's broken nose and boxer's confidence? The world bled with her three times since that first. She understands why her bleeding was called a curse. She needs to leave this place and she needs Elazar and she needs Rivka Mendl to be gone.

She needs a curse. She is Sarah Gittel's daughter and the bitter, stabbing words that had flown off her mother's tongue like black ravens had always been her mother's form of discourse with the world. Words had power; the right words from the Holy Tongue uttered in the right order had made the world and said backwards could dismantle it. But would using them as often as her mother did smooth and weaken them? Besides, which of her mother's curses would root into Rivka Mendl's soul, turn it into ashes, snort it away through her nostrils? She did not have patience to wait for a whole or the next *shvartz yor,* black year to descend on the bitter, hungry widow. Should she utter a spell to compel her to go shit in the ocean, *gey kacen affen yam*? But who knew from oceans in Kolno? And anyway, the experience would seem to be a pleasant voiding: clean, salty sea water and gentle minnows caressing one's bottom in contrast to *kacen* in the dark outhouse, through its wood-splintered hole and clouds of flies. And besides, these days whenever her mother commanded her to go defecate in some body of water, Raḥel would glare in resentment at Sarah Gittel, thinking, and sometimes saying, it was what they should have done on the ship to America on which they had not sailed. Perhaps her father would have uttered those words when he had withdrawn his arm from the sleeve of death and pointed to the moon, to America or whatever land lay beyond the ocean they would shit in before arriving at their destination. Now she dreams of making that voyage with Elazar, passing through borders that were merely dreams, nebulous as spider webs. Now she needs not a stick but a curse, for Rivka Mendl, who will keep Elazar here, who will keep him from her. None of her mother's curses seem appropriate. So what if Rivka Mendl *zolst du vaksen vee ah tsibele, kohp in dred,* grew like an onion with her head in the ground? What good would that do Raḥel? *A soyve zol id dir machn,* may I have the privilege, she thinks, of sewing your shroud.

In the end, she goes to Maja.

This is not like you, child.

Apparently it is.

You sound like your mother.

I need her stone heart.

Maja takes her hands, as if to comfort her, but then seizes Raḥel and presses her face against her breasts, the rough cloth pushing into her mouth.

Przeklac? She uttered the Polish word for curse. Do you see me as a witch, Raḥel? You would curse yourself, child. There is no need. I have seen Elazar's wife to be. She is being eaten from the insides by a wolf. She will not remain long on this earth.

Raḥel closes her eyes and tries to feel what she knows she should feel. It doesn't come. Instead her heart soars.

She asks herself what price she would pay for this rejoicing, what curses had she uttered which would turn back and curse herself?

Chapter Five: Dov's Toes

Her brother Dov had escaped to America years before, when he had received word from a comrade who'd infiltrated the secret police, that he was to be drafted into the army, a traditional way of getting rid of troublemakers.

On a cold winter morning a few days later, he bared his left foot and placed it on top of a stump behind the house. He looked up at the iron gray sky. Then he looked down at the gnarled stump sticking out from the smooth expanse of snow like something mutilated. Leaning against it was an ax. Dov broke the ax from the frozen grip of the ice, swung it over his head in a hissing arc, and brought it crashing down on the ice in the small trough next to the stump. It took two more blows to break a hole through the thick skin of ice. As soon as he saw the black water welling through, he gripped the ax up high on its handle with his right hand, touched the cold sharp blade to the area he wanted to hit, brought the ax up and then swung it down swiftly onto the stems of his two smallest toes. In the instant of the arc he saw himself frozen like a picture: a lean, intense man swinging an ax, his breath steaming in the air. The instant shattered like a shard of ice.

He heard the solid chunk of the ax biting into the wood, felt it vibrate in his palms. He saw bright red blood gouting out onto white snow. The pain seared up his veins and lumped into throbbing, red-hot iron behind his eyes. Lifting his leg with both hands under the knee, he plunged his foot into the hole in the ice, which was already shrinking, then withdrew it. A blister of freezing blood formed around it. He sat on the stump and wrapped the foot in linen, then picked up the two pellets of his toes from the crusted snow. He wrapped them in some fine German linen he and his father had smuggled over the border the week before, and, using the ax for a crutch, limped back to the house.

Months later, after he'd become involved in more radical politics and learned he was to be arrested anyway, he left the village. As he walked away, his mother came running down the road after him, holding the linen packet, screaming after him to take his toes, to take her, that he would need them both in America

Chapter Six: The Boxer

You can blame it all on the girl. But like anything and everything, it is not so simple. If you want to understand the true origins of what Kolno people, with delighted malice call the disgrace (smacking their lips on that word like sweet *hamestashen*) and unforgivable humiliation of Rivka Mendl, I must tell you something of how strange was the connection between her and her husband to be. I witnessed its beginning, in my place, Benya's Gimnazjum Bokserów in Biaystok, where my boxers danced like Hasidim in front of the mirror that covers one wall and saw reflected back at themselves not the roped square and hanging bags and mist of sweat but a dim room of *cheder*, full of dust and shadows, beams of light flickering through the chinks in the wooden-planked walls onto the letters in the books, letters that dance and weave like boxers themselves.

Elazar K, had been one of my best prospects back then, that orphaned letter K the result of having been forbidden by his father to use his family name when he boxed, Herschel, a man with two thousand years of bobbings and weavings and combinations and rules in his own head. A man husked by disappointment and grief, when his wife, Elazar's mother Miriam, died, Herschel made the small house where they had lived into a coffin for himself. Day after day he sat in one narrow room, sealed in darkness, melting into the walls as if he were draining from his own veins. In a coffin, he shrank to a corpse. He tried to pray, but his words fluttered helplessly against the pressing walls and fell around him, dead and weightless. He refused to take money from Elazar. For fourteen hours a day he did piece work for Taubman, the middleman, his fingers bleeding, his prayers humming out from his sewing machine.

Elazar had become a boxer in the army, a talent that had no place in his father's world. He came to me as to a father who could teach him how men prayed in this new age. But when Rivka Mendel started coming to the gym, I couldn't protect him as a father should, I had not the rules to protect him, no more than Herschel. Rivka Mendel, a middle-aged woman, was the widow of Abram Susskind who had left her his tanning business. She was a barren woman, a dry, cracked piece of earth who in her barrenness had given birth to herself as a sharp-nosed crow, dressed always in black feathers of mourning as if for the dead sack of her womb. She stared at my fighters with hungry scavenger's eyes, as if they were her stolen, unborn children. There was nothing I could do. I couldn't keep her away. These were Jewish boys I was training and my custom and tradition was to let my fellow Jews in to watch them so they would draw strength from each other. David HaMelech, it's said, danced naked before the people when he became king. For that matter, Elazar might have been King David; a beautiful boy, tall, his hair a gleaming helmet of tight-red-gold curls. He might have been naked as King David, the way that Rivka Mendel's crow eyes picked over his skin as she watched him spar or work the bags or skip rope, her mouth opening and closing silently, little extra lips of white spittle hanging at its corners. Her head moving in quick, crow jerks.

I couldn't stop her, but I didn't need her, didn't need the *tsouris*. Elazar was getting ready for his fight with Tadeusz Bareja, a Warsaw fighter who was known to be a member of the anti-Semitic Black Hundreds. It was said that during the university ghetto-bench riots, when Jewish students demonstrated against quotas and segregation, he had participated in the rape and murder of a Jewish girl. It was the kind of match that would draw everyone, Jews and Poles, and Elazar was nervous enough about that. Everyone meant Natan Lepke, the gangster, also. Lepke waited for Elazar like a hole in the earth waits.

Before he had gone into the army, when he was seventeen years old, Elazar had seen Lepke do the worst thing in the world. That was Lepke's weapon; he let everybody know he would do the worst thing in the world, even though by doing it he would put it out in the world, like a choice that could happen back to himself. Then he would do it anyway, that's the point. Lepke knew that most men are like the kind of bad boxer who holds back his punches and makes a truce in his own head, hoping his opponent will hold back also. But Lepke never held back the howl in his wolf's heart, and he saw, or wanted to see, that same quality in Elazar. From the first time he saw Elazar fight, Lepke was hungry for him in the same way Rivka Mendel was hungry for a child.

Not that Elazar was such an innocent child. He had done jobs for Lepke commensurate with his talents: punishing with his fists and feet several men who welched on gambling debts with, or loans from Lepke, and had threatened to do the same to several shop keepers who felt they could do without Lepke's protection. Then one day he told Elazar to bring Little Mojzesz Tartikoff to a construction site. Little Mojzesz was an organizer of gambling games and a taker of bets who had been infringing into Lepke's territory. He had not wanted to come. Look, Elazar told him reasonably, we'll go together, you'll take a beating, you won't do it no more, life will go on. Elazar believed what he was saying because he wanted to believe it. Little Mojzesz believed him because he had no choice.

When they stepped through the fence, Elazar's hand on the small of Little Mojzesz's back, Gurrah Szapiro stepped out of the shadows to meet them, and Elazar saw Mojzesz's hand shaking, the little man so weak with fear he gave Lepke's lieutenant his trembling hand like a bride going to her wedding dance. So weak, Gurrah had to pick him up under the arms, his body's waste flowing down and out when he was lifted, Gurrah cursing him and lowering him quickly into the metal barrel, pushing Little Mojzesz's head down so Mojzesz was kissing his own knees, his nose in his own stink. They could have done it quick, but Elazar hadn't been brought there because Lepke wanted him to see something that was over quick. Elazar felt Lepke's stare on his skin like dirty fingers. He was strong, a hitter, but he wasn't what Lepke thought he was. He kept his eyes pinned to Little Mojzesz and saw Gurrah knock the lid into place, its metal touching Little Mojzesz's neck, his screams growing fainter and fainter, as faint and as effective as Elazar's father's prayers, fading as they put the barrel into the hole in the ground and buried it. We bottled Little Mojzesz, Lepke laughed.

Later, as soon as he could, Elazar came back to the construction site and he dug, using his hands like a dog going after a bone and when he opened the lid he saw Little Mojzesz's neck was worn right to the bone where he'd worked it back and forth against the inside of the lid nubs of bones gleaming like the teeth of a secret smile at him in the moonlight, the barrel almost half filled with shit, as if Little Mojzesz had tried to dissolve himself. Elazar imagined him in the barrel moving like his father, like Herschel, in prayer, in darkness. He knew he was supposed to be hard about Little Mojzesz until he was worn to the bone inside himself and that was how men prayed in the new Poland. But he felt the darkness Lepke had put around Little Mojzesz wrapping around him like a black tallis. That was why he came to me. He knew, he thought he knew, that Lepke let my fighters alone; they were all officially in the Maccabi League, all in that part of the world Lepke didn't seize but kept free to amuse himself with chance.

Never mind he wasn't so right about it. I made some agreement to Lepke about Elazar's purse money that broke my own rules, so for a while I knew Lepke would be happy about that. So Elazar was OK for that while. Until Rivka Mendel began showing up at the gym. Day after day.

Benya, he said to me, shifting, looking at his feet, that old buttonhole looks at me like I'm something she wants to button.

Looking ain't gonna hurt you. People look at fighters. That's what you get paid for, Elazar, I told him.

Come here, he said, and I followed him to his locker. We walked under the harsh hanging lights, through the staccato of blows and grunts, the sharp wafts of sweat-smell, me watching myself walk after him in that wall of mirrors that opened to another Benya's, a world in reverse. Elazar opened his locker door. I'd always taken a kind of pride that from the filth of his house he'd come out an immaculate kid, his locker always clean, clothes folded neatly. So now I was shocked to see how the order had been destroyed, the inside of his locker a damp confusion of towels and socks and trunks.

Look at this, Elazar said, reaching in and pulling a small white box from the mess. He opened the lid. Inside was a gold wristwatch. It gleamed from the dank darkness of the locker like a treasure in a cave. Every day for the last week, he said. Something Different. A ring, a vest. And no note, nothing. But I know who sends.

You don't know it's her. Lots of fans around . . .

Elazar punched the locker door.

Take it easy.

I'll tell you what she did, this sad old broad. Yesterday, she comes to me with a *shadchan*, a matchmaker. Comes to me like I am my own parents and asks for me like I was a bride.

He drew a gleaming white linen scarf from the locker, pulling it out like a magician doing a trick. He threw it on the floor and ground it under his foot. I picked it up.

It's good material, I said.

Soon the story about the matchmaker got out. If Elazar wasn't Elazar, he'd have been a laughingstock. Even then there were jokes. Nahum Rubenstein, a pretty heavyweight with no sense, gave him a whistle and a pinch on the behind as Elazar walked into the gym the next day and Elazar pivoted like he'd been waiting weeks for someone to make that move and dropped him like a sack. Nahum was never pretty again.

Those days and nights of Rivka Mendel's courting, sitting alone in the darkness of my office, I began thinking for the first time in years about my wife Chana, blessed be her memory. How we had been introduced in the old-fashioned way also, through a *shadchan*. It had brought a sweetness of anticipation to our lives. We both knew if I showed no strangeness we'd inevitably stand together under the canopy and lie together in the marriage bed. That waiting was a sweetly edged hole in me I knew would be filled. I'd look at Chana talking or laughing or putting food on my plate at her parents' Shabbos table or bending over to take up the dishes, actions I'd seen women doing all my youth of wondering at the secret flesh of women and I'd ache wonderfully with the knowledge of inevitability, that I would follow custom and this girl would wrap into my most secret dreams of longing, come naked to my nakedness, to my dreams that waited to burn in her flesh. So that when she came to me that first night and laughed wildly with the freedom of her own dreams her laughter was the freed dybbuk of my secrets. Her laughter delighted me even as it troubled my spirit, even as Rivka Mendel, a woman who'd gone to a matchmaker, an old buttonhole trying to fill itself, troubled my spirit. We are soft as cloth, I thought. We fold into spaces. We walk through the mirror and reverse. The glass of the mirror sticks only for an instant to your skin, like the water of memory.

Such were my crazy thoughts in the darkness of my office. So when I heard the whisper of voices I thought them just more whispers from my mind. But someone cursed sharply and I realized it was from the gym, where no one should be. I slid my desk drawer open and slipped the gun I kept there into the side pocket of my cardigan. I didn't think I'd need it. Fear of Lepke kept petty thieves and Polish hooligans from the gym; the only intruders I usually got were neighborhood kids come to touch the glory. But I was already uneasy that night and the weight of the gun in my pocket comforted. I opened the door quietly.

My office fronts on the catwalk that hangs above the floor of the gym. I slipped off my shoes. Cat walked.

But there was no need. Neither of them could see me, so intensely were their eyes fastened to each other. Elazar in his boxing shorts, his hand up in a defensive stance, as if the white box Rivka Mendel was holding up to him was a punch about to be delivered.

Stay away from me, you crazy bitch.

The only light on in the gym was from a dim bulb in the ceiling. I could see her smile and her black eyes in that light.

Look, Yankyev, she said, using his Yiddish name; I ain't so bad, she said, a reasonable voice coming from that smile and those eyes, like she'd swallowed a real person. Where you going to do better? You going to let people hit you like a bag the rest of your life until your sense pisses out of your *kopf*? Her voice went wheedling. My place in Warsaw, Hipoteczna Street, middle of the Jewish quarter, someone like you could make miracles. I got buyers out all over the country, Yiden and goyim; the mill owners think we have horns and tails but to me they sell. Buyers wait outside my office every morning like peasants, hats in hand, you'll see. You can sit there like a prince, you want, with strength, or if you want, you don't lift a finger. Only sit there, *leben*, my children waiting in you.

I felt Elazar's shudder in my own heart.

You talk like a crazy, he said.

Look, *leben.*

She opened the box, her crooked fingers scrambling on the lid, and pulled out what was inside. It glimmered red in the red light. She shook it out, held it by the shoulders. Elazar's name was embroidered in gold on the back, in Polish and Hebrew letters. For a second I saw him reach to caress the material. But he drew his hand back as if he'd touched fire, slapped the robe down onto the concrete floor as he had the linen scarf.

Get away from me, crazy. I don't want your gifts.

Rivka Mendel just chuckled, as if Elazar's words were without power. Her eyes ate him like Lepke's eyes ate him and she touched him, his cheek, then down the flesh of his chest. Just a short touch but again my heart shuddered the way his skin shuddered after her fingers and she laughed again, that soft knowing laugh from a vision of the world as strong and certain as Lepke's, so strong that all Elazar could do was cleave himself to it. She picked up the robe and handed it to him again.

She left him standing with it in his hands.

He wore it to the fight that night. It shone with richness but it must have weighed like years on his shoulders. Then he shook it off and grinned at me like David HaMelech grinning at the people, as if he'd already won and I knew in that grin he'd seen me there when she'd given it to him and had worn it just so he could stand in front of me and shake it off. I grinned back and grasped my hands over my head, naming the winner. He came out dancing and the Jews in the crowd got on their feet yelling just as if he'd given them back years spent in the dark moldy wet of little wooden houses, the cages of sweltering tenements, the pressing dark of the sweat shops, all with that little shrug that dropped the robe to his feet. They yelled his name. Elazar, Elazar, Elazar, Elazar, they yelled. Yankyev, Yankyev, Yankyev, they yelled. Hebrew, Yiddish, like a map of the Exile, each name folding him deeper into their names, their secret souls. And then I watched him enter the ring naked to name himself in the world. And his opponent from the other Poland, the other Bialystok, Tadeusz Bareja, came out and his people yelled his name, and I could see in the clearness of that moment like the robe had been shrugged off from over my eyes, their hunger to name themselves and to blot out our names that they saw blackly scrawled on the pure white parchment of their souls.

Bareja was a pale, sharp-faced boy with a nose that wouldn't last if he kept boxing and a rash of bright red, pus-topped pimples against the white skin of his back and chest. I wondered if he'd rubbed filth into his skin to make it erupt; I've known fighters who have done that to make their opponents reluctant to clinch, though I won't allow it from mine. In Bareja's movement to the center of the ring I saw Elazar a year before, a street fighter, wise, tense to dodge whatever the world threw at him.

They touched gloves, Bareja bouncing up and down, pushed by his own raw energy while Elazar stood solid, holding himself to a contrasting idea of calmness he knew would play to the crowd. He smiled at Bareja coolly, like an indulgent grownup, and half the crowd laughed.

At the bell, Bareja leapt halfway across the ring as if released, swinging wildly, all his compressed energy and nervousness exploding into that flurry of fists. It was straight Bialystok street-fighting, all or nothing in the first minutes of the fight, just what Elazar and I had figured from Bareja. Hoped for. Sometimes a boy like that goes far, but it's only because there's no way to read him, no design or formula to his punches, like a maniac gangster who grows fear around him with his murderous unpredictability. How do you debate a maniac? The pattern of his world doesn't fit to the pattern of yours. So Elazar stayed easy, letting the wild blows rain on his shoulders and arms, rocking and bobbing as if in prayer, pulling back just enough to let Bareja's punches fan his face. I teach my fighters about the rabbi who could move so delicately between the rain drops he never got wet and it was this way Elazar moved through Bareja's crazy rain of blows, ducking a little, weaving, throwing in a few series of quick, hard left jabs. Kike fighting, I heard someone yell, someone who got the point. Elazar did also; I could see he'd found the pattern that even Bareja didn't know he had, its openings, the weaknesses of its logic, the crack of uncertainty at its center. He'd found what stitched the madness and he rejoiced in it and his own punches now started to unstitch it and he was lovely in his knowing. He backpedaled slowly, drawing the Polish kid on, taking more of Bareja's blows on his arms and shoulders, some of them landing hard enough and loud enough to bring the Poles to their feet and send our people suddenly silent, with only me seeing Elazar's hard, telling, little jabs. I was behind his eyes like a soul, reading Bareja with him, seeing the slight pause that lengthened just a little more each time before Bareja's hunger drove into his arms and fists again, seeing Elazar write the Talmudic logic of his counter-arguments, his *pilpul,* onto the Pole's consciousness until Bareja knew it was written there. Saw him test it: Bareja's hands dropping slightly and coming up again as Elazar signaled, with a slight drop of the shoulder, a left jab at him that never started but placed Bareja's hands just where Elazar wanted them, as if Elazar had pulled them around himself. Bareja's head turned and Elazar's right cross nailed him straight and clean on the hinge of his jaw and he went down hard, the side of his face smacking the canvas.

For the second time that day, Elazar danced for his people. Arms raised, head thrown back, gleaming with sweat, he danced around the ring, and they wrote his names in sound on that the sweat-stinking air of that Polish auditorium. Stop showboating, I yelled at him, but I was smiling, enjoying when I should have still been serious, still keeping my mind on my business. Which was Bareja struggling to his knees at the five count.

At that moment Elazar's smile froze in a way that

froze my heart. I followed his eyes to Rivka Mendel.

She'd worked her way to ringside and was grinning up at him, her mouth jagged and strangely long in the light and shadow, her arms outstretched, her thin fingers clutching as if she were squeezing his heart. Elazar jerked his head clumsily to the side as if to avoid an invisible blow, his first ungraceful move of the night. I saw his power dissolve.

Tadeusz Bareja was on his feet.

Elazar turned, his dance slowing to a weary shuffle. I made myself look, all of me listening for the bell. Bareja smiled, his teeth showing between his burst lips; it was a smile he'd stolen from Elazar and so was the right cross he threw fast and vicious and he swiveled just right and spun on the balls of his feet getting his weight into it. The crack of Elazar's nose breaking kicked my heart.

I worked on him in the dressing room, ignoring the insistent knocking on the door and the yelling outside. I got him out the back way. When we got back to the studio I did a better job on his nose, stuffing in wadded cylinders of cotton to prop it up. But the fine arc of it had been broken in two or three places and I could feel the gristle of the bone grate sharply against my fingers. I knew his nose would spread a little, then a little more, coarsening the face of his youth. He looked at himself in the mirror, touched himself.

It was a lucky punch, I said, but Elazar wouldn't say anything or look at me. He sat on the rubbing table, the red robe bunched in his lap. I left him alone. I was already a little impatient with him, and I felt an unreasoning resentment towards him, the way I knew the Bialystoker Jews would from then on be impatient with him, without his beauty to give it hope. I went to my office.

I straightened my desk and went over some of my bookkeeping, comforted by the neat columns. It was night and I was alone and felt it. The old run-down warehouse of a building with its decaying brick walls was suddenly the walls of my body. I began to feel badly about how I'd left Elazar staring into his own defeat in the mirror. I closed the light and walked out onto the catwalk. I came quietly down the stairs to him. When I was but three feet away, standing in the shadows, I froze. Again, I saw Elazar lit by the one dim ceiling bulb, alone and standing naked in front of the full-length mirror on the wall and I felt again what our people must have felt when he stepped into the ring, as if the flesh of my own youth, or what my own youth should have been, had stepped out of me. The red robe was bunched at his feet. For a moment he stood perfectly still, staring at his darkened form in the mirror. Then he stepped closer and touched his swollen, broken nose. It stood out grotesquely in the piss-yellow light, a wound on beauty that I knew as I knew my heart nobody would ever forgive him for, nobody but the one who'd gotten what she wanted. He touched his ruined nose lightly, helplessly, then let his hands flutter lightly down the front of his body, lingering, like a virgin's farewell to the privacy of her own flesh. With a quick movement, he reached down and picked up the robe and draped it over himself, caressing the cloth as he had his own skin, twirling in front of the mirror, smiling mockingly, coquettishly, at his reflection like a dreaming bride. I sighed, I couldn't help it, and Elazar turned. A look of terrible understanding passed between us.

Chapter Seven: Two Weddings

In April, Elazar stands under the *chupah* with Rivka Mendl. He had gone along with her wedding plans as if he had boarded a train; let it take him wherever it went. As they stand next to each other, she turns towards him and for the first time he can remember, she looks full into his eyes and blinks at the sight of him, as if he has just been created out of clay. Standing this close to her, he thinks he catches a whiff of dried blood and faint rot. He looks away. *Boiee challah*, come bride. He remembers how her father, who owned a tanning factory, had stank of his trade, tells himself it is the memory of that stench in his nostrils, not something emanating from the flesh of this woman. Her eyes are gentle and liquid as a cow's, as if the spirits of those animals her father had stretched and beaten had lodged in his seed. Jewish funk, the Poles call the tanner-stink. Next to Rivka Mendl, his old boxing manager, Benya, stands frowning and stern in a black coat and cylindrical cap, standing in for Elazar's mother and father. How would they have felt about this day, his marriage to this woman? Would his father, a *melamed,* have welcomed Elazar marrying a widow as a mitzvah? Would his mother be content that his bride would be setting him up in the family's tanning business? He looks at her again, trying to see her through their eyes: Rivka Mendl resplendent in smuggled black silk and pearls taken from the ships of Odessa. Beads of sweat necklace his bride. It is cold outside but the packed bodies in the synagogue heat the air like the interior of a tanning shed; he knows who is being skinned. The tall, arched window on the left wall of the building has been left open. Just outside, framed as if in a painting, he sees the white mare his friends in Bialystok are giving him as a wedding present. The mare had belonged to his friend Dov, gone now to America; Dov's sister, Raḥel, is holding the horse's muzzle reins, glaring at him, it seems, in hatred. She tosses her cloud of black hair an instant before or an instant after or the exact second the horse tosses her mane. Black and white. Elazar's eyes lock with hers. They have been seeing each other, she coming often to the horse market on Senkevitz Street, saying she was there to visit this same horse. They had walked along the river. Once they had bathed in it, Raḥel entering the water shyly, from behind the bush where she'd undressed. The memory burned in his mind. The eyes that stare back at him are as wild as the mare's and as Raḥel tosses her head again, the horse, attuned to whatever was roiled in the girl's spirit, rears up, pulling front hooves from the muck of mud and melting snow, breath steaming white flumes from the fiery red membranes of her flared nostrils. Elazar can't take his eyes off her. He thinks of her brother, Dov, who had mutilated his foot with an axe to avoid being drafted, and then had rode away on another horse to avoid arrest. The chanting of the rabbi weaves into the whinny of the horse, the muscles under the animal's sleek coat twitching as if the rabbi's words had turned into sharp-pointed Hebrew letters that poked under his skin. Elazar feels the skin on his back and buttocks as if it were burning under his heavy gabardine. He becomes aware that everyone, the whole sweating, twitching mass of his people, pressed together, waiting to be skinned, is staring at him as he stares out of the window at the girl, her eyes still accusing him. The rabbi bends and places a glass folded in cloth near Elazar's right foot. Thinking again of his friend who had cut the toes off to avoid being trapped, he shifts and stamps his foot down hard, but to the left of the glass, missing it, hearing the moan from the congregation, the crazed whinnying of the horse, all of the sounds pressing as if with strong fingers at his temples and with the same sensation he knows Dov must have felt as the swing of the axe suddenly released from his fear, he leaps to the window.

Looking back, he sees his people as if framed in a picture: Rivka Mendl's angry red face, the O of Benya's mouth. The congregation spills onto the steps of the synagogue, men and women shouting at him, waving fists. He turns from them. What he sees now is Raḥel's secret smile as he leaps onto the back of the mare. Her face is alight with triumph. *Boiee challah.* Come, bride. He reaches down and she grasps his arm, her fingers tight around his wrist as he swings her up behind him.

Chapter Eight: The Smuggler's Daughter

Clinging to Elazar's back as they ride away, Raḥel closes her eyes. They will go to Bialystok, Elazar, who had plucked her from her life like a princess in a fairy-tale, like an overripe plum, yells back to her. She nods, her face pressed into his back, the smell of his sweat stinging her nostrils. Making the day real. No fairy tale this. They will go to Bialystok. It seems *fitting* to her. She had last come to that city when she was ten years old, traveling with her father, illegal samples of linen wrapped around her, *fitting* warm as an embrace under her clothes, the way she wraps herself now around, fits herself to the hard, solid body of the man bobbing up and down in front of her, as if to keep them both from flying off the earth. Riding again to Bialystok, her mind unwrapping like a loosened bolt of linen.

In the cart next to her father's slim perched form, his secrets lying cool on her body, she lies back and closes her eyes and feels the vibrations pass into her. The wheels hit a rut, the cart leaps from the earth. She opens her eyes and claps her hands over her ears and lets blue sky and rolling white clouds fill her vision; it is as if she is tumbling through the sky.

What do borders mean to birds? She remembers her brother Dov saying to her once: *our father is a creature of the air, little one.* In her mind she sees a tiny black winged form looping on a sky white as parchment, her father's bony face and thin hawk's nose and deeply shadowed black eyes peering down at fields and forests. At home, in the evenings when he would lie down, she would push under his arm the way she'd seen ducklings press against their mother's wings. The soft feathers of his beard would tickle her cheeks. She would hear his heartbeat muffled under the thick velvet of his robe.

At the checkpoint back into the Pale from East Prussia she smiles sweetly at soldiers and custom agents and lets them pinch her cheeks. The cart is empty; when her father is asked what he brought over he says, dried mushrooms, and gives the guards the papers he carries. After they pass, he places his hand lightly on her head and looks at her with a strange sadness. She glows under his touch, but the look and the uniforms suddenly scare her, remind her of the stories Dov had told her about the mounted policeman, Tobie, and his jail at the edge of Kolno, at the edge of the Piska forest. He would bring the smugglers he bagged and clip their wings, Dov said. She saw broken bodies pinned to dark wet walls.

What do borders mean to birds? Borders trench her country, her town, her house, her heart, deep aching ruts: how can she lift above what has been scored inside? On each side of the line she's a different person, a story flowing to the shape of a body, like cloth. *Let Zak go shit in the ocean,* her mother said. *How will you bring the sample to him?*

Magic, her father had said.

They ride into Bialystok a week later, her father tall and calm in his great black caftan, his square linen cap, the hawk-tension of his posture. What country does she live in? Russia? Poland? No, she lives in the country of the Jews. She and papa are surrounded by flocks of black-clad Jews, screeching like crows, wheeling, their faces stamped with the panic of birds that have lost the secret of flight. The air smells dry and rotten as if brushed by a desert wind and the faint whiff of carrion. She clings to her father's arm. She clings to her husband's arm. Young men, shaven Jews, their faces hard and mocking, stand on the corners, yell rhyming Yiddish phrases to her in a city slang she doesn't understand. Young women, their faces painted, wink at her from dark windows. Her father pulls the reins, and they stop and dismount. A fat man in a leather apron nods and takes the reins, touches the brim of his hat in salute. They walk across the street towards a crumbling brick building. In front of it more young men and women perch around sidewalk tables, glasses of tea steaming in front of them, their faces narrow and strained. A troop of street actors, *Kassa,* suddenly whirls through the street. The people on the sidewalks laugh and applaud. Down with the blackleg scabs, screams a boy in a skull mask, skeleton rib-bones painted on his vest. She feels drawn towards the actors, their intent expressions, the outrageous freedom of their costumes. A desire to join them, as sudden and wild as their mad whirl through the street, slips into her heart. It frightens her more than anything she has seen. Her father stands watching for a moment, a slight, knowing smile on his lips that her mind clings to like the safety of a secret place. Her hand clutches his arm.

Magic. She thinks of the hot room in Danzig; how the woman winding the linen around her body had winked at her. Tight and smooth as a lover's embrace, girl; that's the way. She had felt the warm cloth weave into her own skin, felt dizzy with happiness at her father's trust, his wrapping of her to himself. His magic.

The performers drift away. Snippets of conversation float to her ears from the young people at the sidewalk tables. She hears words she had heard in her brother's mouth hatch from their mouths. Agitation, says a girl with glowing green eyes, tossing her tangled red hair. Action, a tall boy, Dov's age, says and winks at her. *Kassa,* he whispers. Suddenly, as if he were a curse called up by the boy's wink or words, a man dressed as a spider leaps in front of her and begins to cavort crazily, his face crusted with white paint, black fangs dripping with venom painted under his lips. Four lifeless but madly bobbing legs are fastened to each side of the spider's shirt. She holds her father tighter. The spider winks at her like the tall boy had, turns and begins dancing after three thin young men dressed in gray webby rags. A young boy with an ash-smeared face laughs and yanks off one of the spider's legs as it goes by him. People applaud and laugh. The spider rips off another leg and begins beating the rag-draped figures with it, chasing them in a circle. White signs suddenly wink through the gathering crowd, more of Dov's words alighting on them. *Awake, Betrayal, Solidarity, Revolution.* The spider hits his victims with his torn-off leg, drives them into a dark alley. In a few seconds he comes scurrying back out, face twisted comically, his victims chasing him and beating him with his own legs. Bloodsucker, exploiter, they yell. *Kassa,* the tall boy whispers to her again. The real under the mask of the real, he whispers. She laughs, filled again with a strange restlessness. He takes her laugh into a series of mocking caws.

Her father's face creases with sadness and disgust. She crinkles her own face in imitation. He turns, gesturing at her to follow, disappears into the darkness of a cave-like entrance inside a small alley as if he'd dived off the earth. Panic scurries in her chest and throat like a thin dusty spider. She plunges after him. *What's a border but a choice?* her brother once said.

The walls inside the dark and narrow space are made of the same stained brick as those outside, but they are furred and crusted with wet-streaked mold, the walls softening and blackening around her as she descends so the light not only darkens but seems to thicken. Particles of mossy dust float in the air, clog her throat and nostrils, make her cough and sneeze. The floor levels. They are in a cave-like room. As her eyes focus, she sees dozens of pale human forms lining the walls, writhing in the shadows, their hands fluttering over the cords that fasten their bodies to what seems to her to be great squares of web. A thumping vibrates and throbs between the close walls like a heartbeat. She covers her ears, but the noise comes through her hands so the skin of her palms trembles against her ears. The figures become skinny old men with stiffly tangled beards, their faces thickened with gray dust, but as she stares some become small, drained children, boys and girls. Young and old, they are Jews who can't fly hunched over sewing machines or webbed into the strings of looms, husked and sucked dry.

A round face smiles at them from the darkness on the other side of the cave. She sees the Kassa spider from the street flowing into his real form, the real under the mask of the real, pale and bloated, gliding towards her past the gray husks of his victims. His hairy white fingers flutter in the air, pinch her father's slim hand.

Zak, father says.

Zak can go shit in the ocean, her mother said.

Nu schoine, Raḥelle, come.

Her father beckons her, his face bony and merciless. Come closer, why do you wait? He unbuttons her blouse. She struggles in his grip. He looks at her in surprise. What's this? Stand still now, *leben,* heart. Her heart is a stone in her chest. Her father reaches into her blouse and pulls out the tip of the linen wound around her middle and begins yanking her out, unraveling her; he is pulling her fluttering soul. She feels it loosen and move out from under her heart, pure and gleaming in the dusty gloom. Zak touches it and sniffs it and licks it with his moist pink tongue. He looks at her strangely.

Your daughter is too old for this function.

She's a baby.

The spider caresses the cloth. She feels his fingers, as if on her skin. Father draws her back, buttoning her blouse thoughtfully. He smiles at her and pats her hair.

Wait outside for me, *leben.*

As she walks, she looks back into the dark in the rear of the room and sees her father and the spider, their figures bending and wavering in the shadows, their faces fluid. Smiles wiggle into frowns, frowns dissolve into daughter. In the dim light under the earth, she sees her father change.

Agitation, she whispers.

She runs, spiraling up to the light of the sky, bursting into the glowing day. The light outside polishes the surface of objects and hurts her eyes. She can't stop the race of her thoughts. Her mind teems with words that scream and shove for attention like the crowds around her. Betrayal, she whispers. Awaken. The city vibrates around her as if shaking itself free of invisible strands.

Chapter Nine: The Café of the Question Mark

Europe becomes a room. The same room. Cramped and cold and dark as a cave. Flowered wallpaper blistered or blotched with fantastic continents, dream portals to places-other-than-this. Peeled in stripes as if someone had clawed at it desperate to enter those countries. A stained mattress on the floor, scrawled with the graffiti of other fugitives. Desperate messages or casual musings or rants written in Latin letters or Cyrillic letters or the barbed Hebrew letters of Yiddish. At night the same flickering candle throws their conjoined, moving shadows on the wall, multiplying it and connecting into the forms of all those other scrawlers. When Elazar blows it out, cockroaches scamper across them and the noise of the street seeps into the room. Carriages rumbling over paving stones, carters yelling, their shouted words teetering on the edge of meaning.

Like two characters in a folk tale, Elazar and Raḥel had jumped on a white horse and galloped away from his intended bride and a wedding that sat like a black toad on their future. They had first ridden to Biaylstok, where he found a buyer willing to pay well for Malka, the white mare. His old boxing manager Benya had arranged, or more exactly insisted on, a quick wedding for the fugitives, coming up with a rabbi, or what Elazar hoped was a rabbi: a cadaverous stick of a man, his strangely yellow-colored hair and beard sticking out in clumps like little explosions around his face. Elazar had heard of him; the gangsters' rabbi, and the only guests at their wedding were three lonytekniks, enforcers, he knew from the Bialystok underworld and Chaim Leikert from the revolutionary wing of the Bund, a group Elazar had also done some work for in the past. He had feared that when Raḥel became more acquainted with the Bialystoker part of his life, she would be repulsed by the sordidness, the threat of violence that strummed under every action and conversation, and would take her feet and run back to Kolno. But she seemed delighted in all of it. Including their love-making, which she took to with an enthusiasm that among other feelings about it, relieved him: he had been afraid she would be repulsed or shocked by that as well. He was ten years and a century older than her, feared a young girl's romantic notions that might have only gone as far as their fairy tale escape from a witch, now shattered by the reality of their human joining.

They had joined humanly all across Europe, and he knew they had to stop or start using protection or they would be carrying a third passenger on their journey. Neither of them had the identity papers they would need. Benya's gangsters had given him the name of the contact in Bern who could help them get false papers and passage from Bremerhaven in Germany to either America or Palestine; they had also helped arrange the means to get to Switzerland. The price was several deliveries he would make for them in some of the towns and cities they wished him to visit, including a packet of diamonds to their man in Berne, a big *macher* apparently, as well as whatever other tasks the man might give Elazar. America waits in his mind like a last room now. He thinks always of her brother Dov cutting off his toes in order to escape the Russian army, like an animal chewing itself out of a trap. He didn't mind smuggling the diamonds. But he is uneasy about the unnamed task he would need to do for the big *macher*, this "connection," as Benya called him, in order to get the papers or money the two of them would need to get to a continent as fantastic in his mind as anything he can see in those blotches on the walls.

When they get to Berne the room changes. Walls clean and white-washed as a hospital. They leave a chalky powder on their skins when they brush against them. Pale blue translucent curtains flap from a large dormer window and caress a blue-painted wooden table. Sunlight stripes the walls, the swirling dust motes in it a new galaxy of possibilities. The bed is a miracle of shining brass, its mattress over-stuffed with down feathers and covered with clean cotton sheets and a spotlessly white comforter. Lying on it, delirious from a fever that seemed to come on him just as he entered this room, Elazar feels he is sinking into the pale breast of a bird.

He awakens to see a thin, pale young woman with skin as white as the walls and straw-colored hair standing next to Raḥel, looking down at him. A gold Russian cross sits in the hollow of the woman's throat, its chain around her white neck. She feeds them cabbage soup swimming with raisins and warm bread that tastes like the eve of Shabbat in Kolno. The house, she tells them, belongs to Russian exiles, Tolstoy Christians sympathetic to the plight of their people. They like Jews, she murmurs. Your suffering redeems them, she says. Her name is Sonya. The house belongs to her parents, rich Muscovites who had maintained houses and bank accounts abroad and now themselves as well; they were in London, leaving her in charge of the house in Switzerland. Actually, they didn't like Jews. To be utterly truthful, they know nothing of her activities, she says, smiling triumphantly.

I need to meet my connection, he tells her. And we need money. Work. For the meantime.

Otto Leipzing, she says. The Café of the Question Mark. Your friends have arranged it.

He goes a few days later, when the fever has subsided. Sonya enjoined Raḥel to stay in the room; she only agreed after they had had their first fight when he lost patience with her stubbornness, though now as he walks through the streets of Bern he wishes she were here to share this with, imagines how she would see it. The city makes him understand how filthy and primitive what he had assumed to be the state of the world—that is, Poland—truly was. Electric streetlights cast warm yellow pools of light on the clean sidewalks, their tall, gracefully curved poles hung with baskets filled with brightly colored flowers. The Swiss strolled with a militant, busy confidence, drumming soft white fingers against the comfortable roll of their bellies. Even though it is night, tall, beautiful women, their hair piled high on their heads, whirled bright parasols behind them as they walked, the colors flashing in his eyes like his fever, the giddy scent of their perfume mixed with the heavy, sweet smell of strawberries and wine that drifts to his nostrils from the open doors of restaurants. People tip their hats to each other. They wear frock coats and linen or silk vests and the women wear embroidered satin dresses, both genders encased in cloth Raḥel's father would have had to smuggle into or through the Pale like gold. He is insubstantial, provincial among these people, a ragged child with a snotty nose pressed up against a bakery window filled with elaborate pastries and cakes. He feels passers-by staring at him uneasily, his sharp, dark features and hungry intentness a knife in a world that rejected sharp edges. There should be different streets for him to travel around this city, a nether world he can slip through unnoticed, like the forests along the border he used for smuggling. A Jew street.

He turns a corner, following Sonya's directions, and there it is, just as she described: a dark, narrow alley, the tops of the buildings on either side seeming to lean in towards each other, pinching the space above. In the left wall, a cave-hole of a door. No words on the small sign fastened above it. Only a red question mark, burning in front of his eyes.

The gray walls inside are scribbled with black soot from the greasy candles sputtering on the tables. The walls are lined with curtained alcoves; where the curtains aren't tightly drawn, Elazar can see figures sitting and whispering, their faces close together, licked by the candlelight. Other faces, sharp-featured, framed by tangled black hair, turn and regard him with narrowing eyes as he walks into the room. A pause, silence and then the patrons turn back to each other and their voices rise again. Their animated gestures and the staccato bursts of Polish, Russian, and Yiddish he hears seem theatrically exaggerated after the discrete Swiss mutter outside. In a café like this in Lomza or Bialystok or Warsaw, every third person would be an informer. Sonya told him that in the past many famous revolutionaries would come to the café, Jews and gentiles. Lenin and Trotsky and Plekhanov. Jewish nationalists and Zionists also: Zhitlovsky, Weizmann, Babel and Feivel; the writers Ansky and Asher Ginsburg, exiles waiting for a country for exiles. Their chattering shadows played on the smoke-stained walls.

A hand clasps his shoulder. Don't worry, pal; you'll fit right in.

The speaker is a barrel-shaped man with a square red beard that hangs like a curtain from his chin. He squints at Elazar from beneath a shaggy unibrow that shades bright blue bloodshot eyes.

Otto Leipzig. Sonya told me you would be coming. Leipzig extends a slab of a hand, shakes Elazar's hand vigorously when he grips it, after a second's hesitation. Come, follow me. I'll get you an apron. Your buddies have arranged everything. Can you work? You're skinny as a branch. Come on, follow me, I'll put some weight on you; do you know how to wait tables?

He realizes the red giant has spoken to him in Yiddish.

Later, when Raḥel asks him what was on the menu of the Café of the Question Mark, he replies: Jews. Debating the future as if debating the choices and possible directions of his own life. Russia, Poland, Palestine, America. Where should we go? What will we do? What should be done? Over here, the communists yell at him, bring schnapps and vodka and sit with us, shake off and forget the chains of the past, and while you are at it, pour what we need according to your ability! Ignore those assimilationist swine, waiter, scream the Bundists, bring it here, stay, don't forget where you come from, build heaven where you find your ass! No, no, over here, yell the Zionists, beer without a table for a table without beer. No, this way, shout the Tolstoians, the Mensheviks, the anarchists.

What are you waiting for, waiter? What are you going to do?

Otto tells him of a famous meeting between Lenin, Trotsky, and the Zionist leader Chaim Weizmann, right in this place years before, when there were even more exiled Jewish students in the city, attending Berne University because of the restrictions on Jews going to Polish and Russian schools. The three came for a drink after a raucous three-day debate at the school, Lenin and Lev Davidovich Bronstein AKA Trotsky against Weizmann for the salvation of the Jewish masses. In their millions, Otto winks, disaffected, disenfranchised, not to mention pissed off, agitated, hungry, murdered, raped, impoverished; in a word, ripe. At the end of the three days, most of the Jewish students signed up for the Zionist organizations. Lev Davidovich had been particularly incensed at the loss, left this place swearing to himself after only one drink with Weizmann, though arm in arm with a female Jewish student, enflamed with a spirit of internationalism. The girl, Otto says, though presumably also Trotsky. Who had taken the rejection of the other student bodies as a personal humiliation in front of Vladimir Ilych, embarrassed as much as if his circumcised Bronstein putz had flopped out in front of Lenin's coldly analytical gaze.

Elazar tries to imagine the two men sitting here, Trotsky gone, the remaining two bald heads and pointed goatees sitting and staring at each other as if each were looking into a mirror. So waiter, what will it be? Over here, Lenin yells to him, bring vodka. Nonsense, bring a nice glass of tea and some marzipan, Weizmann counters, both men profile to profile, each a side of a coin Elazar has yet to flip. Nu, Vlad, how can you equate freedom with erasure, asks Weizmann. How can we give up our name in a world that demands names? As if we could. As if the world would let us. The cruel way we have been carved gives us our form. This waiter and I have paid too dearly for being who we are, to just let it go. I, my dear Vladimir, came from the Pale, just like this waiter, look at him, history is writ on his face. How can I explain to you, my dear future Bolshevik, how the Jews in my own shtetl, Motol of the reeking marshes, live, their poverty, the fantastic and terrible occupations they had to invent to survive it, their isolation from the Polish and Russian masses with whom you wish them solidarity. The fact is, Mr. What-is-to-be-Done, all that links Jews to Russians and Poles is the shifting piece of ground on which they balance themselves and being murdered by them—isn't that right, waiter?

My dear Chaim, surely you see how the Pale of Settlement is a metaphor for Jewish existence, Lenin says pedantically. In between nations, in between classes, *nichstihein, nichstihier*, hated by the peasants, hated by the upper classes, hated by id, despised by ego; we should have invited Sigmund. The abnormal pressure of being in the middle, my dear Chaim, in between forces as it were, purifies and polishes some into gems, into saints and prophets, squeezes and misshapes more into furtive, clannish, scrambling hustlers and exploiters, distorted souls, monstrous shapes, cheapskates, greedy goblins and golems: into the very forms the gentiles accuse you of inhabiting.

Weizmann is nodding, taken by the rhythm of Lenin's words. Yes, yes, yes, my dear Vlad, it is why we must reclaim the space we left, to become a normal people again.

Do you believe it will be different in Palestine, among the Arabs? Why define yourself so narrowly? Does freedom mean hanging onto that? Nonsense. Freedom is liberation, one has to cut oneself off from the past with the stroke of an ax, swiftly and brutally. Look at the rest of Europe, with its histories and names, all those names who in the name of their names are flinging themselves on each other like foaming, demented beasts.

Weizmann nods, sugar and honey from the marzipan sticking to his moustache and beard. You make my argument for me, Vlad. You pretend we have the choice to liberate ourselves from ourselves. The choice itself is an illusion. Your people will never let us be anything but what we are. Jews. In between. Yes, *nichstihein, nichstihier*. Thank you. Only the Yiddish will do, our hybrid tongue. Neither here nor there. In between, never among. You need us to be the diamond in your heart and the garbage you must throw from your soul. You need us to fail at the first and to be the latter so that you can continue to crucify us.

The two bald, bearded heads turn towards Elazar, their eyes gleaming in the darkness of the café.

So, nu, waiter, they ask. What will it be?

In the darkness of one of the private alcoves sits the man he is supposed to meet, Leo Bombas, a Jew of no politics who mocks and mimics the slogans that drift to his ears from the other tables whenever he chooses to hear them. Who is taking his time summoning Elazar, for whatever reason he may have. A caricature trying to look like a character, Elazar thinks. Bombas sits most evenings at his table cutting sausages with a folding knife, a greasy roll of flesh hanging over his soiled collar, another over his belt. Cutting and eating and washing down *trefe* with glass after glass of vodka. His appearance evokes a kind of homesickness in Elazar. He'd known others like Bombas when he boxed in

Bialystok: the Jewish underworld, gang leaders, strike breakers, pimps, and murderers. Bombas' stare darts all over the café, flicking here and there along with the motions of his blade, cutting and gathering young flesh at the tables. A dark-haired Russian girl with green, flashing eyes, a slender blond Swiss-German boy demonstrating solidarity with his Jewish socialist comrades. Sometimes Elazar sees him sitting with one of the fish he nets, a young girl or boy, fresh-faced except for their eyes, which look clouded and dreamy under lids struggling to stay open. Injected, Otto whispered to Elazar, with doses of laudanum. Bombas fumbling at their crotches under the table, his eyelids half-closed also; his expression dreamy.

Tonight he is alone. Sit, he says, pointing to the opposite chair. He pushes it out with his right foot. Elazar catches it before it tips over, sits on the edge of the chair, as if ready to leap away. Bombas peers at him.

Don't look so worried. I won't eat a waiter with my meal.

Elazar puts the bag of diamonds on the table. Bombas picks it up, opens it, sniffs at it as if it's food. And whisks it off the table with impressive speed.

You wanted to speak to me, Bombas says, as if the diamonds never existed.

I've been thinking about a sea voyage for two.

Bombas' cheeks quiver with mirth.

You're in Switzerland, waiter.

If you will it, it is no dream.

Bombas nods. And exactly what is it you dream, waiter?

A ship. Two new names so my wife and I can board it. A new history. America. That's all.

Papers without a man, for a man without papers, that it? How much are you willing to pay, waiter? For such a dream.

Elazar points at the place on the table where he'd put down the diamonds. I was told you would help us.

Bombas raises a thick eyebrow, taps the place, shrugs, as if to say there was nothing there. He cuts a piece of sausage, pushes the point of the knife through it, and pokes it towards Elazar's face. Why are you wasting my time?

You have the diamonds. Should I take them back?

You're a forceful man, how could I stop you? He raises his hand, waves a circle. The café fell silent. How far do you think you would get, waiter? The door? Perhaps. Perhaps you would make it as far as Sonya's flat, 9 Carl-Lutz-Weg, number 23, where your wife awaits you.

Elazar shrugs. Why the threats? Why this *kassa,* this play? You have the diamonds. You know my people in the Pale. You know who I am. Otherwise we would not be in Sonya's flat or have a job waiting for me at the Café of the Question Mark. Otherwise I would not be here speaking to you.

Bombas takes a long drink of vodka and then brings the small bag of diamonds back onto the table, spills some of the gems out, runs his finger through them. Yes, I have the diamonds. They tell me you are an adequate smuggler. From your work here, I can see you are also an adequate waiter. Do you possess any other talents? I understand you are from Kolno.

And Elazar understands this is an interview. He drains his glass, the alcohol warming his veins.

What other talents of mine do you require?

Everyone knows about Kolno's horse Jews. Everyone knows about you.

And Elazar understands there was nothing about him Bombas had not already known when he sat down at this table.

I have a horse, Bombas says.

Congratulations. Are you thinking of smuggling it to America?

I value a waiter with a sense of humor. To an extent.

What will you have me do?

The animal is troublesome. I paid a goodly amount for her, but have not been able to mount her. If you are able to break her, that will be your first payment.

And the second?

We can speak of that later.

Bombas waves his hand. His assistant, a stocky, bald French-Swiss, appears instantly at the table. Bombas the magician.

He knows horses, Maurice.

God help him.

Be here at seven tomorrow morning, waiter. Be on time. Oh, and bring your wife.

Why? She is not part of any of this.

Bombas looks amused. He reaches across and strokes Elazar's face. How can you say such a thing? No matter. Bring her. Just for the company. And to meet my horse. A fellow female's company may help to soothe the beast.

He has never been in a motorcar before and sits as stiffly as he had across from Bombas at the table, the memory of the man's touch, the casual, possessive brush of those sausage-like fingers still on his face. Raḥel, next to him, squeezes his hand excitedly, her hair streaming out behind her as they leave Bern and drive into the Swiss countryside. Bombas, massive in the front seat, looks back at them and smiles benignly, the good uncle taking them on a family outing. He sports a feathered cap and improbable lederhosen, his dimpled knees and quivering thighs hairless as slugs. He should look ridiculous, but his size and the slightly ironic twist of his mouth have an effect as menacing as it is bizarre. Or perhaps, Elazar thinks, as menacing because of that self-aware bizarreness. Maurice, driving, wears dark goggles, a brimmed cloth hat, and a leather coat, too heavy for the weather. He doesn't glance back at them as he drives.

They wind into a valley between grassy green hills that farther north grow into snow-capped mountains, the countryside somehow artificial to Elazar, as if conjured by Bombas as backdrop to his ridiculous costume. At the thought, he sees a herd of sheep spill like cream over the crest of a hill, herded by a darting dog and a shepherd, yes, in the same embroidered suspenders and short pants worn by Bombas; the figure even wielding a shepherd's crook. Maurice turns right, onto a dirt road, the dust from it pluming behind them, and they stop in front of a small brick cottage next to a stable constructed of uneven, gray-weathered planks and streaked, mossy shingles, some of them flapping up and down in the breeze, applause at their arrival.

The pasture surrounding the house is unkempt and wild, spotted with evil-looking clumps of thorns and berry bushes. A tall, black-haired women with mad yellow eyes stands in front of the door. Maurice turns off the motor and Elazar hears a metallic rustle of leaves as the wind thrashes the overgrown meadow. And under that sound, a wild whinnying.

Children, meet Lillian, Bombas says.

His housekeeper? His wife, his whore, his slave, his captive dybbuk? Bombas doesn't say. His Lillian, enough name for a new creature, apparently. Her eyes, he sees, are not really yellow; just what should be the whites of them, yellow as old parchment, their corners red-stained from broken capillaries, her pupils black as the jagged crown of her hair.

They get out, stand awkwardly before her.

Do something, Lillian spits at Bombas, and then cringes, though he did not react at all. The cringe turns instantly to a smile, a frown, a cringe again, settles back into smile. She reaches out and strokes Elazar's cheek and then Raḥel's, the gesture mirroring the way Bombas had touched him yesterday. Raḥel stares at her and laughs, delighted at her improbable fluidity. Are we tender enough to eat, she asks.

Come inside, Lillian hisses at her, come, come. We'll have some tea, you and me.

Bombas holds up his hand. First Argamaka. Why you are here, waiter. Smuggler. Horse Jew from the land of Horse Jews. The Centaurs of Kolno.

They enter the stable. Inside is tight and dark, with room for only one stall, the ammoniac smell of horse shit stinging Elazar's nose, making him homesick. The interior is only lit by the daylight coming through the open door. Bombas enters, clutching Sonya's shoulder. Heat and stink. Shit, horse sweat, and congealed fear. Lillian crowds inside. Maurice has taken off his jacket and rolled up his sleeves. The top buttons of his shirt are undone, revealing a chest as bald, or as shaven, as his head, the glimpsed flesh tattooed with a necklace of eyes. Both the eyes in his face and the eyes on his chest stare at Raḥel. Bombas' fat, white fingers briefly touch her neck. She laughs nervously and jumps back. The mare's hooves pound against the stall door.

Maurice opens the door. Argamaka rears up, eyes rolling white, shakes her head violently, flicking white gobs of slaver back onto her black hide. Her halter is fastened with long chains to both sides of the narrow stall. Elazar stares, sick to the soul; the animal would have been beautiful if not so starved, ribs pushed out sharply, black hide lacerated with unhealed cuts, some dripping pus, and a cicatrize of scars. The floor of the stall is thick with droppings; their odor stinging his nostrils. He turns to Bombas, who is reaching over to stroke Raḥel's neck again; as she steps back, frowning, Elazar seizes the man's fore and middle finger, bends them back. Rot in a black pit, Bombas. Bombas smiles at Elazar even as he winces in pain. Horse Jew, he whispers. In the corner of his eye, Elazar sees Maurice moving towards him. Bombas raises his other hand and the Swiss stops. Lillian comes up next to Bombas and begins to fondle his crotch. Bombas throws back his head and laughs, imitating the mare's whinny.

You see what I mean, waiter. A wild Cossack horse. What can I do? Even Maurice, who knows horses, can do nothing with it. Isn't that right, Maurice?

Bombas whinnies in the horse's face.

Get away from her, Elazar says. If you want me to work with her, get out of here. You agitate her.

Bombas nods. Come, ladies, the waiter has ordered us away.

My wife stays.

I'm staying as well, Maurice says. For a second,

Elazar thinks to insist he go. But it doesn't seem worth the confrontation.

Bombas leads Lillian out, his arm draped over her shoulders, his other hand fondling her breast. Maurice and Raḥel move back a few steps as Elazar steps forward, his eyes fastened to Argamaka's deep brown liquid eyes. He can see the horse's soul cringe, alone in the face of madness. She sniffs, nostrils flaring—they have been ripped by a bit and are bleeding—and rears up again, as if to assure Elazar she has not been broken. I know, darling, I know. *Boiee challah.* Come, bride. Argamaka's ears twitch; she shakes his head back and forth frantically, but stills when Elazar lays a hand flat between her eyes.

A hand on his shoulder. He steps back. Argamaka rears again, hooves flailing the air. Elazar turns and looks into Maurice's eyes. The man nods, as if in approval.

She takes to you. She is a good horse, used to belong to a man who took good care of her. It won't take much to bring her around. I could have done it. I've done it before.

So why not now?

Maurice shakes his head. Once she's gentled, Bombas will either ride her to death or whip her to death. It's what he does with any Cossack horses he gets his hands on. He has agents buy them up for him. If you can, Jew, steal a look at the well in the next pasture. No, not at. Look into it. If you can stand the smell.

They look at each other for a moment. Maurice reached over and touches Elazar's right arm, the swell of his muscle.

Do you think, horse Jew, that the only price for your ticket will be this horse?

Bombas made it clear it wasn't. But without details.

Maurice says nothing. Elazar waves at the stable.

Why don't you clean up all this shit?

The door opens. Bombas steps inside, next to Raḥel. She stares into his eyes, her mouth set.

You've had enough time. Have you introduced yourself, waiter?

To keep an animal in this condition is a crime, Bombas.

Hold her for me. I want to kiss her lips.

As if understanding, Argamaka rears, eyes frantic, spittle flying.

Bombas laughs. Wild. Cossack wild. It's in the blood, yes, waiter? The beautiful blond Christian child missing, the sudden increase in matzah production? Once upon a time, I had the acquaintance of some Cossack poets. *Jews bake matzah, we fry meat,* they would sing; they wanted, you see, to help out some grieving Poles, felt the usual rapes, hangings, shootings, guttings too limited for their artistic, poetic natures. Threw a family of Jews into a well, threw in oil and wood, cooked 'em up. My family, maybe, who can remember such occasions? Jew stew for you, the Cossacks sang. Strummed their balalaikas, stroked their moustaches, waved their sabers. These dashing figures on horseback.

A terrible story does not free you to do terrible things, Raḥel says.

Ah, the wisdom of the fathers. *Pirkei Avot.* Or the mothers. *Pirkei Emot.* Do you know what it made me, that terrible story? Hungry. He licks his lips. Does hunger free you, waiter? To do terrible things? That's the question, waiter. How much will you pay, for the gift of America?

He puts his arm around Raḥel, squeezes her right shoulder,

Take your hand off her, Elazar says.

Of course, of course. Be calm. My tattooed friend here—Bombas points to Maurice—is reluctant to help me in this matter. He feels able to refuse, believes I need him too much for other matters. Perhaps he is right? We will discover that together, yes, Maurice?

Maurice shrugs. As you say.

I say this to the waiter. To the horse Jew. Calm this beast for me, horse Jew.

Wait, he says to Bombas. Watch.

Again, he puts his hand, palm flat, on Argamaka's broad forehead, the hair bristling under his palm, feeling the horse's twitch slowly stopping. He whispers again in her ear; she nuzzles against his face.

Raḥel is smiling at him; he grins back at her, they are of the same mind. He will jump onto Argamaka's back and once more reach down for her, his bride: is this horsey exit always to be their beginning? He knows it is impossible. The horse is in a stall, chained, their three strange hosts stand between Argamaka and the barn door, and Bombas next to Raḥel, in seizing distance. A fairy tale ending, a dashing gallop into the sunset could only happen once. He squints at Bombas and Maurice and Lillian, trying to see them as a choice, as figures in a yellowing photograph, as frozen in his mind as a memory.

Chapter Ten: Argamaka

Raḥel remembers the look that had flashed between herself and Elazar in Bombas' stable, the sweat from his fat hand on her back soaking through her shirt, into her skin; both of them had looked at the horse Argamaka, the vision of their escape from Rivka Mendl occurring, she knew, in both their minds. Even as they knew it was impossible. Even if they could both get on Argamaka, get the horse out of the stall and get out of the stable, past Bombas, Maurice and Lillian—a creature Raḥel had come to think of as some kind of female golem Bombas had constructed for himself—where could they gallop off to in that unknown countryside?

They stay at the farmhouse for five days, Elazar working with the horse, but always keeping her within his sight, Bombas staring at her as if she were an anticipated bite of herring on a plate, and Maurice and Lillian, both armed with revolvers, watching everyone. Bombas kept up his façade of humorous menace, alternately jovial and avuncular; grinning like a wolf as he promised huge payments for Elazar's work one minute, patted her *tokus* as if she were another mare he would possess when Elazar's back was turned.

On Erev Shabbat, Bombas calls them for dinner. The farm table is covered with an embroidered white tablecloth and laid with gleaming silverware, delicate china plates filigreed with a design of winding fig vines and figs, crystal wine glasses, and silver candlesticks. Five places have been set. A feast for my Kolno guests, Bombas calls to them. He is wearing a long white robe and a square white cap, the garments a rabbi might don on Yom Kippurim. His cheeks and lips are shiny with grease, as if, Raḥel thinks, he has pushed his face into meat, gnawed and shook it like an animal. To Raḥel, everything, even the fig vine design on the fine china, seems permeated with malevolent mockery. She hates this man who rubs filth into her memories of Friday evenings in her house with her father, mother, brothers and sisters, the glow of the candles softening the harsh angles of her mother's face, even her eyes gentled as she moved her hands in circles above the candles, reciting the blessing. She suddenly yearns for that home, for Kolno, hates herself and hates Elazar as well for tearing them away, even as she knows how unfair that is to him, how unfair it is to herself.

They sit. Bombas lights the candles, gestures to Lillian. *Boie, kurvah.* Come whore. Stand and bless the Sabbath. Lillian stands uncertainly, waves her hands wildly, making the flames dance and then go out. She sits, drains a glass of wine.

Ah, the Queen Sabbath has come. Do you see, he asks Elazar, what I must deal with, with this stupid *shiksa*? He reaches across the table and slaps her. Idiot. Goat. First we must say the blessing.

He re-lights the candle, picks up his cup, and chants Hebrew words that hook like and tear barbs into Raḥel's memory. *Baruch atah Adoni Elohanu Melech Ha'Olam Borai Pre Ha-Gefen. Blessed are You Lord Our God who has created the fruit of the vine.*

Maurice, he calls. Comprendez-vous? We're drinking the fruit of the fucking vine. Bring out the rest of the meal; my Sabbath Queen and guests want to celebrate the end of another fucking week and the taming of another fucking horse.

He reaches over and slaps Lillian again. Get up, my queenie. Get your ass up and go help him.

As she rises, he sings the first verse of the traditional Sabbath Song, his eyes fixed on Raḥel:

Eshet chayil mee yimtza. Who can find a woman of valor? *Eshet chayil mee yimtza verachok mi'pninim michra:* A woman of valor, who can find? Far beyond pearls is her value . . .

Maurice and Lillian come out of the kitchen, each carrying a tray laden with patties of of gefilte fish, gleaming white and seeming to quiver in the flickering candlelight. He places one portion on Raḥel's plate, one in front of Elazar, one at Lillian's place, and the last at his own, follows with a dollop of red horseradish on each. He sits as Lillian comes out. There are five additional fish patties on her tray, each as big as a small loaf of bread; Raḥel is not surprised when she puts them all in front of Bombas.

Our guests, Maurice. What must they think of us?

He picks one of the portions in his hand and sings the second verse, still staring at her: *Batach ba lev baala Veshalal lo yechsa.* She repays his good, but never his harm, all the days of her life. She seeks out wool and linen, and her hands work willingly.

And devours the fish, burps loudly, groans.

Eat, my guests. Eat and celebrate with me.

He smears the rest of the fish loaves with red horse-radish, picks each up in turn and consumes it, smacking his lips. Raḥel feels her very skin tighten on her bones, as if it feels the threat of those teeth.

Why aren't you eating, he asks her. Do we need more blessings? More food? He waves at Maurice and Lillian. Get your asses up. Bring in the rest.

They pile the food on the table. Matzah balls floating in rich chicken soup, the surface undulating with rings of grease. Roast chicken, cholent, dumplings. Bottles of sweet wine and vodka. Raḥel picks at her food, unable to tear her eyes away from the way Bombas devours whatever is set in front of him, the grease on his face glistening in the candlelight. She feels nauseated,

Eat, drink, my darlings. Did you go to *cheder,* horse Jew? I was a *yeshiva bochur,* a young student of Torah and Talmud, can you believe that? He touched the sides of his head, right, left. Forelocks around my head like two dangling cocks. Arguing *pilpul.* Rabbi Fat-ass said this, and Rabbi Little-cock said that. Did Yakov wrestle with a man or an angel or the Big Boss himself? Does the word wrestle mean wrestle or struggle or being there or dust or gefilte fish? Was he given the name Israel because he wrestled with Elohim, or because Elohim broke his ass? Blah, blah, blah, all day talking about one word. Until I wanted to vomit words.

I love *pilpul*. I think it is beautiful, Raḥel says. She had no idea she was going to say those words until they sprang to her lips, drawn from the well of memory, the warmth of Erev Shabbat at her parents' home her mind has conjured against Bombas' perverse feast.

Bombas nods vigorously, jabs a drumstick at her. Of course you do. You're a woman of valor.

Why don't you take your mouth off her now, Elazar says.

Bombas swings the drumstick to point to him. Then let's speak about you, waiter.

I've done what you asked with her, Elazar says. Argamaka is a fine horse. She still needs to be fed carefully and the medications and poultices I spoke about applied. Maurice can work with her from this point; she is gentled enough.

The drumstick jabs. You are a talented horse Jew, horse Jew. And an indifferent waiter. And an adequate smuggler. But it is time to talk about your other talents.

I have a talent for leaving.

The least of your talents. I understand you were a boxer. And a soldier. And sometimes the Movement had need of those talents.

Why don't you take your mouth off him now, Raḥel says; Elazar's words good for her purpose as well, why not? An image appears to her, chills her: Bombas' mouth sucking at her husband's forehead.

The woman of valor, Bombas says, chants: *Gemelat'hu tov velo ra,Kol yemay chayeha darsha tzemer ufishtim, vatas bechefetz kapeha.* She is like a merchant's ships; from afar she brings her sustenance. She rises while it is still nighttime, and gives food to her household and a ration to her maids.

He turns back to Elazar. A *boevik*, he says. A thug. You were in a *shrek-otriaden*, a fright-gang, intimidators, enforcers. Tell me, did your duties as a *boevik* go beyond beatings?

Why this game, Bombas?

Answer me or this game is over.

I never killed, if that's what you're asking. Except in the war.

How beautiful for you, waiter, that you were able to keep your purity. But tell me something: What use to me is purity? He smiles at the words, sings them in a high-pitched voice, strange and disturbing for a man of his size.

Oh of what use to me

Is purity?

Tell me, your wife. Is she pure as well?

I won't tell you again to keep your mouth off her.

And she parrots your phraseology. How disappointing.

What more do you want?

To give you what you want, of course. America. The land of gold and dreams. You have helped me with a troublesome horse. Now, *boevik,* you may help me with a troublesome man. A horse and now a man. The price of your ticket.

Elazar says nothing. Raḥel holds her own tongue.

This last task, *boevik.* And then you will be given the papers you need and you may leave and put water between yourself and me. Water so wide you can drown your memory of us in it. Your memory of the occasion. We won't be real to you anymore, none of us will be. We'll only be a story.

You'll be real to me.

The price of your ticket, Bombas had said, ticket not tickets. She remembers that fat hand squeezing her shoulder, understands the piece of himself her husband is being asked to sever in order to free himself from the trap of his life. Would she cease to be real to him anymore also, only a story from a distant land on the other side of the sea?

Elazar rises from the table. Come, he says to her. *Boiee Challah,* she thinks, Come, bride. Shouldn't his reaction be to put his rough hands, his *boevik's* hands under the edge of the table and flip it over? She sees him tense. She almost misses the glance between him and Maurice, the slight shake of Maurice's head.

Elazar sits. He raises his glass, toasts Bombas. *Le-chayim.*

Bombas starts to raise his glass. He smiles, burps, farts, and slumps over, his eyes fluttering. His face goes into his plate. Lilian stares at him, alarmed.

Liebchen? She starts to rise. Maurice draws out his revolver and points it at her. She snarls, snatches up her dinner knife and he whips the gun against her jaw. She falls as if her limbs had turned to rubber.

Raḥel flushes, relief flooding her and then shame with it. She feels a need to reach across and touch her husband, run her finger over his forehead, as if to write her name.

Thank you, Elazar says to Maurice.

You don't know how to drive, do you, Maurice says. It's a statement not a question.

I can learn quickly, Elazar says. Or you can come with us. He looks back at the two unconscious figures. A trickle of blood from Lillian's mouth was pooling on the floor, Bombas still snoring and farting. Either way, we should move quickly.

He won't wake. I laced his food with more than enough opium. I'm not going with you, waiter, I'll be taking the car. I want you to take something else.

When he led them to the stable, she sees that Argamaka had been saddled.

She's gentled enough, thank you, horse Jew, so I could get that on her. But she still will not let anyone but you, and I hope, her—he nodded at Raḥel—on his back. You take the same road we came on, another twenty kilometers, and you'll be at Basel.

He hands Elazar an envelope. Your payment. A transport fee. Follow the directions inside, bring her to this man.

What will he do with her?

Why is that your concern? He smiled. No, don't worry, horse Jew. He keeps her for me.

And then?

And then what? You're on your own. Get out of the country.

Through Germany . . . Elazar says, like a question.

Try not to be Jews.

Maurice, you can't leave him here alive.

Is that an offer?

If you wish, Elazar said. But he can't live.

Maurice shrugs. As if that were obvious. Or as if it was none of their business.

Why are you doing this for us, Raḥel asks.

He planned to kill your husband, after your husband killed for him. There's more than enough room in the well. You, he would have kept alive, for a time.

Why are you doing this for us, she repeats.

He reaches up, places his hand on Argamaka's head. She snorts, pushes against his palm.

For you? I'm not doing it for you.

Chapter Eleven: Horse Jews

for Isaac Babel

When Rahel's brother Dov had fled Kolno, he dreamt of horses. Wild and snorting, flanks quivering, breath spuming, they ran through his nights as he ran through his days so he woke feeling more tired than when he put his head down. Twice, before the war, he had accompanied shipments of Polish horses sent by the horse dealer Supchik to buyers in Germany and Russia; jobs reserved for only the best riders among the Kolno Jewish youth. The horses, nervous and skittish at the train journey, would calm when he spoke soothingly to them, clucked at them, touched their twitching flanks. Together they'd look at the alien country flickering through the opening in the planks. As later his sister and the husband he would never meet would do, he slept in the box car, curled on straw and pressed by horse flesh; the steam from their sweat, their breath warming him.

He was often feverish or light-headed from hunger, and when the darkness came in a strange city he felt himself losing the edges of his form as if he was dispersing into breath. In his dreams, he galloped across plains bright with blue flowers. On the trains, just before arriving at his destinations, he'd curry the horses' flanks as if scraping away their old lives. He had torn himself free from the inevitability of his life and was neither here nor there, *nichstihein, nichstihier*. The words echoed in his head, sometimes a soft canter of hooves, sometimes harder, the clatter of wheels against rails. *Nichstihein, nichstihier*. The classic choice, the family anthem. But he felt cut loose from all the commitments of his life: family, politics, religion, even the need to make choices. He'd cut himself free. He drifted.

Not long after he'd left Kolno, an old woman in a small hamlet had spat at his feet and crossed herself when he'd come to her door asking for bread, a little water, and he'd been hit from behind and woken up bound and on his back near the village well. The blow had been so hard he'd been shifted into detachment. He watched a flock of geese flying, the black V rippling through the white sky so that at first the black line of horses seemed to separate and emerge from sky, the horses growing larger and into their shapes and his heart swelled for here were all the horses of Kolno he'd fed and tended and whispered to coming for him in a luminous cloud to sweep him away from here and into the sky and he didn't move and now they were close enough he could see the streaming manes and long black and brown faces, flaring nostrils, specks of spittle flying, hooves flurrying the white dazzle of snow into a webbing mist so the horses were concealed and broke through the white membrane again and now he could see the long lean faces of riders, their white breath spuming into the mist. Rifle shots cracked in the air. Screams came from the village. Tongues of flame licked at the sky. The village crackled. A bald, stooped Cossack in rimless spectacles was holding a skinny pig up by its snout, fingers in each nostril, the pink body stretching towards the weight in its hips, the feet kicking. The Cossack carefully slit its throat. The old woman who had spat at him was lying in the mud with her throat cut, another pig working at her frantically with its snout, grunting and slurping at her neck and he looked away, not disgusted but because he didn't believe in the balance of perfect justice. A thin Cossack reared up next to him and dismounted from the back of a roan stallion as if he were unsheathing himself. He drew a saber and cut the bonds, but kept the point pressed.

Why were you trussed? The thin Cossack asked in Russian. Are you a gift?

I came looking for food. They might have thought I was a spy. They knew I was a Jew.

Are you a spy for us?

I don't know who you are. I think you're a dream.

On the contrary, we're the Ninth Cossack regiment.

He laughed. The idea that these apparitions, instrumentalities of his tilted mind, were numbered struck him as hilarious. The flames eating the village leapt around him like madness, crackling with his laughter. The horses whinnied.

Of what army? he asked. The army of dreams?

Exactly. We're red cavalry.

The roan lowered his head and looked at him with its wise liquid eyes. It nudged him gently and whinnied softly. He kissed the horse's warm forehead.

The thin Cossack smacked his lips as if something tasted good.

That saves you, he said.

Chapter Twelve: 40 or 8

Elazar insists they wait until dark to enter Basel, and even then dismount and lead Argamaka in. We'd be a parade, he says. Two Jews on a horse. One of them too beautiful not to draw stares. He means, Raḥel knows, the horse. The way she feels, travel-worn, rump-sore, stinking of her sweat, his sweat and Argamaka's, drained by the witness of murder, she doesn't disagree about which of the two females on this strange honeymoon is the more attractive.

The address where we are to meet Maurice's contact, you know how to get there?

Yes, if that was where I wanted to get.

She stares at him.

Help me with this.

She hooks her hands under the straps and helps pull as he shrugs out of the pack. He puts it on the ground, opens the flap and draws out a white linen bag. She knows what it is. He opens the neck and scoops out some of the diamonds, lets them run out of his hand back into the bag. They make a sound like whispering.

I'd prefer to make my own travel arrangements for us. Quickly. By now, he'll miss these.

She hasn't stopped staring at him. It is as if she needs to memorize this new form into which her husband had shifted, in case he changes so rapidly again. She starts to ask him when, how, he had found, retrieved the diamonds from Bombas without Maurice finding out, but the question doesn't pass her lips. What is the difference? Argamaka tosses her head and whinnies. Raḥel watches Elazar reach up to touch her face, comfort her and then she understands he has not changed at all.

You didn't want to give her up, she says. It is not a question. You want to be a parade, to ride back into Kolno the way we rode out. Is that the picture in your mind?

What if it is?

Are we a folk tale, husband? She is suddenly furious.

Perhaps we are.

She raises her arm, pinches her flesh as if to show him here is a real person.

He puts a hand on her shoulder. As if to gentle her, she thinks, and shrugs out from under it.

Yes, he says, I want to keep her, she is mine: you're right. But it is also the safest way for us. How could we trust Maurice?

He pats Argamaka's rump. You know what I do. I've transported horses from Kolno all over Europe; I have connections who will help us.

You trust them?

Some are friends, so yes. Some are from the Bund, so yes. He touches Argamaka's rump, and then the bag of diamonds, as if to say and there is this.

So now we are thieves,

Elazar sighs. Do you know what these would be used for if they remained in Maurice's hands?

The same activities they would have been used for in Bombas' hands, she thinks, but does not say. Above her head, the horse, the damn horse, whinnies again. She points at the diamonds.

Why go home? Why not use them to get us to America? As we planned.

That door is closed to us. For now.

She starts to protest. But knows he is right. They are hunted, have no papers, no names. America, she has heard, is the land of the free. But it is not the home of the nameless. She still doesn't trust all of her husband's motivations for this change of plans. But she cannot fault his reasoning. And she realizes something else: when her tongue meant to say

Kolno it had said home. She is very tired. She wants to go home.

Nu, she says. So meanwhile while you make your *connections,* we what? Check into a hotel with your bride? She nods at Argamaka.

Elazar grins at her. What else? It's our honeymoon.

A flight of rickety stairs hanging like an afterthought against the side of a building, its green plaster walls pocked with wounds of red brick. This Jewish slum in the underbelly of sparkling Basel, she thinks. Waiting in the dark piss-stench of the alley holding Argamaka's reins as Elazar climbed the stairs. Placing her hand flat between the horse's eyes, as Elazar had taught, the horse's shudder moving into her palm and up her arm, joined with her heartbeat. Proud in spite of the fear of her acceptance by this picky behemoth; she is certain Argamaka has taken her as Elazar's other mare; they are sister-wives. *It's our honeymoon.* Look at me, *Ema,* mama, see how far your daughter has come in the world, sister to a horse. A Kolno Horse-Jew at last.

By midnight, she is sitting on straw in a makeshift horse stall, one of four in the boxcar she, her husband, and Argamaka now occupy, along with two other mares. Destiny fulfilled. The stalls were just crudely constructed partitions; the planks she runs her fingers over are rough, newly-cut, not planned smooth. From where she sits, she can see the numbers 40 X 8, stenciled on the wall above the sliding door. Meaning, Elazar had told her, forty people or eight horses. Or cows, she supposes. Or three horses and two Jews. Try not to be Jews, Maurice had said. The straw isn't protecting her boney behind from the hard wooden floor. At least there are only the three horses and themselves. They have their own stall. The height of luxury, she tells her husband. She had never liked her mother's sarcastic tongue; now it seems she has inherited it after all. Did Sarah Gittel ever have to be a horse?

Hours before, Elazar had come down the creaking staircase next to the alley where she and Argamaka waited followed by a black shadow which, when it got closer, resolved into the form of a Hasid: long black frock coat, fur streimel hat, long *peyot* dangling from both sides of his head. An odd *connection*, she had thought. A religious Bundist? Perhaps it was a disguise. Whatever else he was, the man remained a shadow, leading them through back ways to the Basel Centralbahn, to this boxcar.

Not a Hasid nor a shadow then. A conductor.

They sit in the darkness now, with just the occasional

staccato of hoof beats against the floor, a few whinnies. When they had entered, Elazar had made his peace with the other two horses, and had brought them to each other as well. And introduced her, Raḥel, as well. The other two mares were older, gentled.

She, on the other hand, is just weary.

It will be like this, Elazar whispers. First to Berlin. Meir—he must be the shadow, Raḥel thinks—has already telegraphed ahead to our contact. We'll, the whole car, will be switched onto a Deutsche Reichsbahn train to East Prussia. We'll ride all the way to Konigsberg, about nine hours, and make our way over the border from there. It's a route I've used before, though usually the other way around.

Sitting in a boxcar?

Of course not. But we can't ride in the coach. Maurice . . .

I understand. She lays a finger against his lips. She can barely make out his face in the darkness, but she hears the fatigue in his voice. She feels a sudden wave of love, pure love for this man, flawed as he is, love *because* he is flawed: no longer perfect in her eyes, no longer the shining god coming out of the river, but this sharer of this strange journey that had become their own country, not Poland, not Palestine, not America, but the walls of this boxcar and the rails under its wheels and her father's cart and all else that has brought them here. She leans forward and kisses him.

The car lurches forward. Almost at the same moment, she hears shouts and then someone is pounding on the doors of the other cars, sliding them open. Elazar pushes her down into the straw and leaps to his feet. She sees that he has secured the sliding door with an iron bar laid in its track between the edge of the door and the wall, but he stands gripping the U-shaped handle with one hand, another iron bar in the other. She rises to help him just as the pounding reaches their door. It holds firm. Someone is screaming outside, the words muffled. The horses are whinnying frantically, Argamaka rearing and pounding her hoofs against the stall door. She hears another, metallic noise, metal ratcheting into metal, and her husband suddenly pushes her to the side, pushes her down and lays on top of her. She can see wood splinters erupt from the door as the bullets penetrate it. One of the mares screams. Like a human being. Like the scream of a child. She hears, feels, the thump as its body hits the floor. Please, *HaShem*, not Argamaka. The train starts gaining speed, the reverberation of the wheels under the floor moving into her body, Elazar still lying heavily on top of her.

She runs a hand quickly over his body, realizing he

is doing the same to her. He is intact. She struggles out from under him, her thoughts on Argamaka. But it is one of the other mares, a sway-backed roan whose sagging belly and gentle eyes had moved Raḥel when she first saw her. The other mare stands still in her stall, as if dumbfounded. Argamaka still keeps rearing up, her hooves pounding the stall door. In the corner of her eye Raḥel sees Elazar sticking one of his fingers into one of the bullet holes in the door, muttering something, and she gets to Argamaka first, speaks softly to her. She reaches into the feedbag and takes a handful. As the horse's front hooves come down, she gently pushes her hand up to Argamaka's mouth, the way she had seen Elazar do it back at Bombas' stable. Feels the warm wetness of the mare's tongue, the snorts of her breath against her hand. As Argamaka eats, Raḥel reaches up and places her other hand gently on the horse's forehead. It nuzzles against her palm. When she turns around, she sees Elazar standing perfectly still behind her, smiling, his eyes shining.

Later that night, when they are sure they are somewhere in the German countryside, they open the boxcar door and between the two of them manage to push the carcass out, along with the straw that had been befouled as the horses had opened their bowels.

*****

The train rocks her to sleep. As if she has managed to board a boat to America. The mare's soft snorts and whinnies seep into Raḥel's dreams. Argamaka dreams as well. She bursts out of the walls of the stall pressing all around her and now she is running over the endless empty plain the wind entering her, pushing her, the earth solid under her hooves, and dust rising around her. She runs with the rising sun towards the far horizon, and there is nothing around her but grass, glowing and delicious and brushing against her belly like the caresses of a thousand fingers and she is the rising sun, the light moving with her to illuminate the dark earth that smells like joy in her nostrils. Suddenly she hears the thunder of the herd around her as they catch up, tossing their manes joyfully, welcoming her back, their hooves beating into the earth that pours its strength through their hooves, all of them around her, her sisters and brothers. They are running to a point on the horizon which, as she draws closer, clarifies into the stall she had just fled; as she comes to it, still galloping full speed, its mouth slides open and she slams inside, the rest of the herd pushing her inside following and now inside the smaller box and its walls rise around her and the others press in with her; it cannot fit all of them, this small space, and yet more and more horses press inside with her, surrounding her, their flesh pushing against her flesh, harder and harder as more gallop into the small space, until their hides press against every inch of her, even into her eyes and mouth so that when she tries to rise she cannot because of the weight of them, and when she tries to see, she cannot because of the press of them, and when she tries to whinny she cannot because they press even around her mouth, and Raḥel is on the ship, rocking gently, the rumble of waves vibrating in the metal under her feet; she sees her mother tearing off her hair and tossing it into the sea just before she is pushed by the press of people around her out of the light and into the foul-smelling darkness of steerage as more and more people, they are all Jews, peyot flapping, shawls tight around faces, more and more Jews press her down, surround her, push in so tightly she is even breathing in rises of their flesh plugging into her nostrils and on the wall she sees a metal sign that says forty or eight in Yiddish and now the steerage hold itself shrinks around her, around all of the bodies pressed against hers, smaller and smaller and the rocking of the ship becomes the rocking of the train and the metal walls of the ship's belly the inside of the boxcar and Argamaka's whinnying penetrates the dream and wakes her.

She sees Elazar, his face pressed against the narrow gap made when he must have opened the sliding door a little. His body is nimbused in a red glow that spills past him and plays against the inner walls. She rises, still feeling the weight of the bodies from the dream. It falls from her as she walks forward to join him. He moves aside a little to let her see. They are passing through a small town of gingerbread houses. As the tracks take them near its square, she can see a mob of people, men in brown shirts, red armbands, some carrying torches, the flickering of flames alternatively illuminating and then darkening their faces into distorting masks. The flames from the torches and from the building on fire at the edge of the town square, the Star of David over its front door licked by flame. She and her husband watch as the flames fade to a spark and then to blackness as the train continues to Konigsberg.

Chapter Thirteen: Homecoming

They ride into Kolno on the back of Argamaka, keeping their faces expressionless and staring straight ahead. Argamaka, as if sensing their mood, the eyes trained on them as they come up Lomza Street and turn onto Zabielo, holds her head high, tossing it arrogantly now and then. They feel a bit ashamed of themselves. Their parade. But they have pictured and spoken about this entrance since Basel, all the miles on the train cramped in a horse stall. They had left on a white mare; they return on a black mare. Unspoken between them was the hope their fairytale entrance would be entertaining enough to distract people away from the cruel way Elazar had left Rivka Mendl under the wedding chupah.

As they hitch the mare to the post in front of the Brikman house, Sara Gittel emerges, looks at them, her face twisted in disgust.

Why didn't you go to America, you and your gangster?

Her anger is not, as Raḥel expected it would be, so much sparked by what she and Elazar had done, but by the journey they had failed to complete. Her father had wanted her to leave, to put an ocean between herself and this place.

She finds her mother is not the only one who felt that way. Those who didn't ask that question, thought it anyway. Many of the Jews and some of the Poles regarded her and Elazar with stony anger. Rivka Mendl had died of throat cancer soon after Elazar abandoned her at the *chupah*; of course he was blamed. Perhaps he blamed himself, Raḥel sometimes thought, though she never said it aloud, that her words shouldn't bring that curse on herself. Though she would eat any curse, if it were the price she had to pay to have Elazar. But she could see that even though people feigned indignation about the way Elazar had left Rivka Mendl standing open mouthed under the canopy, inviting the cancer that would fly into her throat, what disturbed them the most was that she and Elazar had not finished their escape to the Promised Land. People felt as if their own dreams had been shattered, and blamed the two of them. Why didn't you go, they asked, as if their own feet were caught in mud.

Because the ticket cost too much, was Raḥel's reply to everyone.

When he had learned of Rivka Mendl's death, Elazar

closed his eyes and kneaded the flesh between his eyebrows, just above his broken nose. That poor old woman, he said. But in any case, Rivka Mendl had no living relatives and had been widely disliked, particularly by the tanners who worked for her, who had been paid too little, worked too many hours, and were nagged too much by the woman. And Raḥel and Elazar's escape, as they had hoped but never said aloud--the way he had galloped off with Raḥel like a wild Cossack and a year later returned the same way—had become a romantic legend that the young Jewish girls, and a few of the Polish girls as well, whispered and giggled and dreamed about. Or hated or feared, as if either such escape or such return was a rebuke to their lives.

Shortly after they return to Kolno, Raḥel goes to her father's grave for his blessing. Sara Gittel refuses to go with her. Should I share your shame with your father, she asks.

I'm sorry, papa, Raḥel thinks. I'm sorry we did not sail away into your dream. She remembers Bombas, shudders. The ticket would have cost too much, papa. She places two stones to mark her visit to the grave. Feeling like a stone herself. A small stone called to a gravestone as if to envision the form into which it could swell. A Jew bringing another Jew to Kolno.

Kolno takes them back. It is what Kolno does, Raḥel knows. Raḥel wants to believe. It is what Kolno did when her family came, wandering westwards away from the pogroms in Russia or eastwards after the massacres in Germany after the Expulsion from Spain after the Expulsion from Judea after the Expulsion to Babylonia after the Exodus from Egypt after the Exodus from Canaan. As she and Elazar, no longer expelled, settle into the family house on Zabielo Street facing the market square, vacant except for Sarah Gittel, she feels herself trying to settle also into the stream of that history. Something she had never felt the need to do before. To feel that her life had precedents and context. To learn the wisdom of wandering and the wisdom of staying.

There were other ways they could have tried, she supposes, to obtain documents and passage to America. But after their own fraught wanderings, the word "settle" seems exactly the right term for her mood. They had failed to reach the Promised Land. They are lucky to be alive. After murder they crave mundanity.

When they finally disembarked at Konigsberg, she felt only relief, embraced by the familiarity of the landscape.

After Switzerland, after Germany, Kolno, with its pattern of cobblestone and dirt streets that lay like a soft grid furrowed into their minds, its thatched or tiled roofs and elaborately carved wooden shutters and lintels, its wavering desert chants leaking into the Polish air from the plastered brick walls of its synagogue, its river and the deep shades and dappled light of its forest and the golden fields that surrounded it as if it were an island, its lively market square, its horse traders, carpenters, glaziers, blacksmiths, locksmiths, bakers, butchers, tailors, bristle makers, plasterers, raft men, tanners, smugglers, boeviks, scholars; its Hasidim, Mitnagim, Cabbalists, Zionists, Bundists, communists, beggars, thieves, writers, saints, madmen and maniacs, its galloping, stomping, snorting, rearing sweat-flecked horses whose personalities and peculiarities seemed to reflect those of the human herd around them, its Brikmans and Lobels, its aunts and uncles and cousins, its warren of intricately linked and known relationships as much mapped in their navigation of the world as its streets, had replaced the dream of America in both their minds. They had come home.

A year later, when the Poles opened a gymnasium that allowed Jews, even Jewish girls, to attend, she took classes, though when the authorities found there were three Jewish students to each Pole, they evoked the *numerus clausus* restricting Jewish enrollment and closed the school. Marshal Pilsudki, a sometime protector of the Jews, had died, and many people were nervous, feared the resumption of pogroms, a fear reinforced by the events in Germany. Later, a new *melamed,* teacher, Chaim Szapiro, who had taken over the cheder after the death of Elazar's father, opened a Beit Yakov: a school where girls could study the *Tzena Verena,* the women's Torah, written in Yiddish. It was funded by donations from American Jews who'd immigrated from Kolno, including her brothers. Raḥel had returned to Kolno with a hunger, a need to understand; she felt acted upon, a feather blown here and there, and she didn't like it. At first, she had been afraid to speak about it, the way she felt herself bursting out of her own skin like a chrysalis, with Elazar, but he had just laughed. I've been waiting for you, he said, for the woman I saw in your eyes when I looked down from that horse on our wedding day.

He had encouraged her learning; somehow even getting her mother to begrudgingly accept this new daughter who had come back from Switzerland. What else she had learned though was millinery, a skill she felt her mother appreciated or understood more than the urge to read everything she could get her hands on. Her clever fingers. The Waksul family had opened a small hat manufacturing factory, just one building off the market square, near her house. She had gotten piece work there, but also had liked to look through the catalogs and magazine advertisements for ladies' hats. At home, she had purchased some fabric, feathers, scissors, and other tools and created two hats to her own design. There was nothing she could do with either the hats or the skill in Kolno, where both Jewish and gentile women wore shawls, but when she showed what she'd made to the owner, Shmuel Waksul, he'd been taken enough to offer to buy the design, an option she not thought possible. The hats made to her specifications had sold well in Warsaw and other large cities, and Waksul had paid her for more designs. She loved the sense of creating something beautiful from what first seemed like random, disconnected pieces of nothing. She liked making money from it also—the idea of making money doing work she loved also a new notion. She dreamed of her own hat factory, one day, perhaps. Her dreams quivered fragilely over a sea of nightmares.

Meanwhile she kept reading, not only the *Tzena Vere*na, and the older writers like Peretz and Shalom Aleichem and Chava Rosenfarb, but also secular novels and the newspapers and literary journals coming from the capital with work from a new generation of authors who wrote in Yiddish: Janusz Korczak, Julian Tuwim, Jan Brzechwa, and especially Bruno Schulz. She drowned in Schulz's stories, his words opening a floodgate of images in her mind, somehow magically evoking what she could feel but not say, all forming from the same Yiddish she could use every day to buy a chicken. She had begun to have long conversations with Szapiro. She was not the only woman, or girl, with whom he spoke about Torah and Talmud, always reminding them of the importance of the *emot,* the Mothers, Sarah and Ruth, Miriam and Esther the other women who had saved *Am Yisroel,* the People of Israel. His lessons to the girls had led to complaints to the Kehilah, the Central Office of the Jewish community. It didn't seem to bother him. He shone, Raḥel thought. As with Elazar's father, even some Poles would come to him for advice or judgement.

She and Elazar and a few of the other young Jewish families indulged in the modern fashion of celebrating the Christian New Year's Eve, drinking wine and enjoying the feeling of being fashionable. Until someone set off fireworks. Their noise and flashes pushed memories of other times in this market square into her mind. Sarah Gittel just nodded at her, smiling slightly, as if to say: see what you get? She didn't join the celebration. She would wait, she told them, nine more months until Rosh Hashanah, which would come in its own good time on the first of the month of Tishrei, in the year 5700, or September 13th, 1939, as the goyim reckoned time.

Chapter Fourteen: The Dybbuk

Chaim Szapiro, the *melamed,* sits with Raḥel, Elazar, Yitzhak and her cousins Beryl and Rivka Radowski outside Beryl's shed in the market square, drinking fiery plum brandy. Rivka raises her face into the sun as if squinting at the bright dawn of a New Day as she proclaims the Dictatorship of the Proletariat, necessity of. She, Beryl, and now to Raḥel's surprise, her own yeshiva-bochur little brother Yitzhak, have declared for Marx and Lenin. Though Raḥel suspected his true God was not Marx but movies, a newer obsession for him.

Beryl, a blacksmith, has set up the shed displaying harnesses, saddles, lariats, and other equipment, on the assumption it would be easier for Polish farmers to come here to buy such goods than in the horse market. A good capitalist, thinks Raḥel, for such a communist.

Elazar and Beryl light slim, black cigarettes, offering one to Szapiro, who declines, and losing another to Rivka who reaches over and extracts it from her husband's leather pouch. Beryl just grins at her, lights it, watches her expel plumes of smoke through her nostrils. A bit much, Raḥel thinks, but then thinks why not, and takes a cigarette herself, glancing at Elazar to gage his reaction. He doesn't seem to have one, but she knows he is skilled at that. At not reacting. She inhales the smoke, the taste harsh and bitter, imitates Rivka's casual exhale, enjoying sitting there, the image of herself sitting there.

A reader of newspapers and journals now, she knows that poverty has descended on Kolno like—in the words of Karlinus, her favorite Warsaw newspaper columnist; he writes for the *Haynt*—a dark blanket. Poverty and enmity between Jews and Poles, back more strongly after the death of Pilsudski, a defender of Jews, and exacerbated by resentment that many of the Jews are helped, as her family is, by the American *gelt* sent by relatives who seemed to be supporting half the town. As well as nervousness among the Jews about the events they have been hearing or reading about in Germany. But around her, she sees the market place teeming with people determined to ignore both politics and poverty: Polish farmers and their wives here to buy supplies or decorations or to have equipment repaired, mostly on credit, or selling grains, vegetables, or charcoal from stalls or carts; other Poles from town as well, including a tough youth gang from Lomzer Street, the *Schkotzim*, but mostly

Jews, mostly young and mostly dressed in modern rather than traditional clothes, there to see and to be seen, talking, laughing, eating and drinking, listening to a ragged Klezmer band in from Krakow, arguing with speakers from the different political groups.

Argamaka is tied to a post behind Rivka, the mare's black mane an echo of Rivka's wild crown of black hair. Her flanks are flecked with droplets of sweat that glimmer like jewels in the sun. A shimmer of muscle moves like a current under her sweat-sheened black skin, moves into Raḥel, awakening an ache of lust for her husband, who is tossing his own head in unconscious imitation of the horse, laughing, his sleeves rolled up on his muscular forearms, his boxer's hand resting on his friend's shoulder.

A small group of Poles, led by Basil Dombrovski, the local leader of the Endecja, the anti-Semitic Polish nationalist party, slowly walks by the shed. Dombrovski stops, lifts up one of the harnesses, as if to test its weight. One of the Endeks snorts, and a titter runs through the group, as if in response to some secret joke. Raḥel recognizes the snorter as Yankayitis, a dour, balding man who had become director of the Polish school and pushed her and the other Jewish students out of the door. Jew bastards own every shop or business in this town, he mutters. He and Beryl lock eyes. Elazar smiles at Dombrovski, speaks in Polish. Good day, Pan Dombrovski. Can we interest you in a saddle? Or perhaps a whip?

Fucking Red, Dombrovski says, with an exaggerated Yiddish accent.

Her husband looks back at the goods in the shed in mock confusion. No, I'm sorry, Pan; no fucking red for sale here.

Argamaka neighs behind him, snorts nervously.

That a horse like that belongs to a Jew is a crime, Yankayitis says.

Elazar draws on the cigarette, blows smoke in the Pole's direction. She's no Red either, Pan, he says. Votes solid Bloc of National Minorities, every time.

Yankayitis sneers. Says: As if there's a difference.

Raḥel feels the tension between the two groups like an electric current. They lock eyes with each other, except for Szapiro, who smiles benignly.

The group moves on.

There's your proletariat, Elazar says to Beryl.

Proletariat? Yankayitis won't know a working man if one hammered a nail into his *pupik.*

May they hang by their tongues, Raḥel says.

I was in Kyiv when the Third Army took it, Elazar

says. Later, Pilsudski apologized for what Polish soldiers did to the Jews there. Only he said the abuse was not done by Poles but by the Polish-American volunteers who had come to fight. He said that it was because in America they didn't like beards. Anyway, such things happen in war, he said. Pilsudski.

Anti-Semitism is a disease of nationalism, Beryl says.

In the Soviet Union there are no anti-Semites? Szapiro asks. That man hates you for being a Bolshevik; for him Jew and communist are the same. But the Red Cavalry also slaughtered Jews. For being Jews. Perhaps you're right. In the Ukraine, your Stalin starved equally millions of all nationalities and religions.

Propaganda, Rivka says.

Szapiro continued as if she'd never spoken. And your Marx, your prophet, he will cause the lion to lay down with the lamb, swords to be beaten into ploughshares, yes? How miraculous.

Beryl takes a long swig of the Slivovitz and a long drag on his cigarette, and shakes his finger at Szapiro.

Tsk, Rabbi, what kind of rabbi are you? What kind of holy man?

I'm not a rabbi. I'm a *melamed*, a teacher.

A rabbi isn't a teacher? Do you remember that dwarf who taught us, Yitzhak?

Always, Yitzhak says.

What was his name?

Gedalie Ali. Always.

Now that was a pious man, Rabbi.

No doubt.

You should join us, Rabbi, *melamed.* Beryl fingers the sleeve of Szapiro's caftan. Discard the medieval clothing and the medieval brain. Discard Jerusalem for Moscow.

Discard *HaShem*? Discard that joy, Szapiro asks, smiling.

And the cabalistic nonsense, Rivka added. This number is worth this number is worth this number.

Yes, join us, Beryl says again, grinning widely.

Stop tormenting the man, Elazar says.

Nonsense. It's all in good humor. And comradeship. He knows that, don't you comrade Rabbi? But truly, you should join us. You spout *pilpul* as if its dialectic. You're a progressive person—you teach women, you believe in the equality of the sexes, the bourgeoisie hate you.

Rivka laughs, raises her glass.

Enough. Stop torturing him. Raḥel snubs out the cigarette.

Beryl downs another shot of Slivovitz. Szapiro, laughing, matches him. Beryl slaps the table. And you drink like a Russian!

No, Beryl, and you my dear Rivka and Yitzhak, Szapiro says, you should join us. Come back to your people. You sprout dialectic as if its *pilpul.* You wrestle with the universe, even if you won't call it *HaShem*. You believe in goodness and justice. He reached over and patted Beryl's arm. And in spite of your wonderful proletarian muscles, you argue like a Jew. I will continue to say the Eighteen Blessings for you. You have a Jewish head, a *yiddische kopf.* Yes, and you also, Rivka. In keeping with my reputation for encouraging the equality of the sexes.

And what about me, Raḥel asks, sipping the brandy. Do I have a *yiddische kopf,* Rabbi?

You, my dear, more than anyone. You bring passion to whatever you set your mind upon. You are open to the world. At the same time, you won't tolerate its nonsense.

Beryl laughs so hard that Slivovitz explodes from his nostrils. Do you hear how this man talks to your wife, Elazar? Bringing passion and so on?

Don't you recognize Talmudic commentary, comrade Blacksmith, Elazar says, slapping Szapiro on the back, laughing. He gets to the heart of her, our scholar, while

I still struggle to read the complex text she is.

Her husband.

Beryl frowns. To her heart he gets? He seems concerned with all our wives, this teacher. Why is that? Where is your wife, *melamed?* Who has ever seen a *melamed* without a wife?

For a moment, Szapiro says nothing. He looks away from them, looks around the market square.

Are you searching for an answer, Beryl asks. Or for a wife?

I'm searching for Jews. Szapiro gestures at the crowd of sitters and walkers and shoppers and sellers. Look at the Jews here, blacksmith. Which are the Jews?

Beryl frowns at him, then laughs. Better to ask who isn't. He points, there, there, there. Yankyev, that idiot, Mokzesz, Naum . . . all within ten feet of us? Or do you just mean the women?

Naum. How do you know he is a Jew?

How should I not know?

Take away the caftan, the streimel, the *peyot,* he has the face of a Pole or a Russian. How did Naum obtain that face?

Nu, Beryl says. And so the subject of a missing wife is lost to an obscure question.

There have been pogroms here?

Have there been floods here, fires here, storms here? Is this even a question?

Yes, you're right. There have been thousands of pogroms. During and after the war. Even until now. Thousands of deaths. Brutal deaths, people tortured, burned alive. And raped. And raped. Always, with each pogrom. Not hundreds, but thousands. As if the goyim *putzes,* their cocks, were weapons to destroy us. Swords. Who will turn cocks into ploughshares, Blacksmith? I've read that in America, many of the black ones, the *schvartzes*, are lighter in color than others; they carry in their veins the blood of the white men who raped their women when they were slaves. Hence Naum, and hence many Naums, the rapists' blood mixed with our own. Naum, whose mother or grandmother or great-grandmother, lived. Unlike other thousands of women, our women, who were raped and then murdered, or raped and then went insane. Who howled at the walls when their men tried to touch them. The asylum, for instance, in the town I came from, Zhitomar, filled with such women who lost their minds. Whose minds tilted, from unearned shame, so they could no longer face their men, no matter how much their men told them of their innocence. Or who took their own lives, unable to live in such a world, unable to stop feeling soiled and stained.

For a moment, no one speaks.

Melamed, Beryl starts to say.

Be quiet, fool, his wife says. You have your answer.

Which, Raḥel thinks, now hangs over them like a pall. Like a dirty blanket. Like the world.

It is her husband who brings them back from the edge of that black pit, turning to Yitzhak, her quiet little brother.

What do you believe in, brother-in-law?

I believe in Fritz Lang.

This prophet I don't know, Beryl says.

Ignoramus. He's a film director. A German, Rivka says.

The year before, Yitzhak, who had already trained and worked as a photographer, had taken a short course in Bialystok to learn how to operate and maintain a projector. He had seen films in that city, and became fascinated by the art, had even worked for a time photographing the group of artists and writers making a film of S. Ansky's *The Dybbuk.* Elazar had given—lent, though there was no talk of being paid back—the money to buy both a projector and a reliable generator, and an abandoned barn near town where Yitzhak had been showing films, leased from a distribution company in Warsaw. He put in benches, a screen made from a white sheet, charged a few kopeks for admission. Tithed much of any profits he made to the Party, out of belief and the hope the donation would keep him from being criticized for being a capitalist. Like the factory and the apothecary and two cafés, the theatre, The Alhambra, as he insisted on calling the barn, was a sign of how much Kolno was changing. Both Jews and Poles had been coming to sit in an uneasy alliance for an hour or two of dreaming when awake, escaping the news poking their eardrums like sharp needles about the upheavals and events in Germany and Russia, the weight of those giants always pressing on the sides of their heads as if they were in a tightening vise.

I believe in Sergei Mikhailovich Eisenstein, Yitzhak says.

Now you're talking, Beryl says. *The Battleship Potemkin.* Lang, whoever he is, has slain his thousands, but Eisenstein his ten thousands.

But most of all, I believe in Shloymi Zanvi Rappoport, Yitzhak says.

Who?

Ansky. S. Ansky.

The folklorist? The would-be bard of a dead culture?

I know you worked on that movie, my dear comrade

projectionist, Beryl says. My dear capitalist swollen toad of a theatre owner. But your Ansky, your Shloymi-Fhloymi Rappoport, whatever his name was, is ridiculous. As is his name. I've seen your *Dybbuk.* He exoticizes us; presents Jews as if we're the savages, the bare-titted South Sea Islanders shaking their grass skirts in that American movie you showed.

Mutiny on the Bounty, Yitzhak says.

He was a fucking Socialist Bundist, your Ansky. We need to erase the borders between peoples, not encourage their tribalism. We need to lose this strange gutter language of ours and learn to speak Polish or Russian.

Not make films in it, Rivka adds dutifully.

Elazar raises his glass and his voice, bursts into the Jewish Bund's anthem. Written, she knows, by the same Ansky. Sung in loud, proud Yiddish, she knows, to provoke Beryl and Rivka. Her husband.

Brothers and sisters in toil and struggle
All who are dispersed far and wide
Come together, the flag is ready
It waves in anger, it is red with blood!
Swear an oath of life and death!

The fuckin' dybbuk guy, Beryl says. Schmaltz and superstition.

Rahel had seen *The Dybbuk.* She could appreciate *The Battleship Potemkin.* Sitting on an uncomfortable bench—next to Elazar when she could get him to come—in the drafty barn, she has also seen Fritz Lang's *M* and *The Cabinet of Dr. Caligari,* though most of the townspeople, Jews and Poles, stayed away from such films, preferring the Americans: *Tom Sawyer, Frankenstein, Shanghai Express, Queen Christina,* and yes, *Mutiny on the Bounty,* which, watched during a snowstorm, made her long for a tropical Pacific island paradise, exoticized or not. But Yitzhak's love for *The Dybbuk*, she understood. She had watched the film with him, her short, skinny intent little brother, just the two of them in the barn, sitting on the front bench. Every bench in the Alhambra was packed for the American films, even though the stretched sheet of smuggled linen hung from rafters would occasionally billow out and distort the images projected on it when wind gusted through the barn's plank walls. But when Yitzhak obtained *The Dybbuk*, he brought her by herself to the barn. To the Alhambra. As if to a synagogue. Ansky, he told her, had never lived to see his play made into a film. This film, we worked on it as if he was there, as if we were possessed by his wandering soul, his dybbuk, he said.

She was taken by the acting, by the haunted singing, the words from the Song of Songs, the actors who did in fact seemed possessed as they played the parts of the possessed, the mysticism and charm of the story itself. *All creatures are drawn to the Source of the Divine Being. In these migrations it may happen that a wandering soul, a dybbuk, enters a human being which once it loved . . . .* But what affected her most was seeing slivers of her innermost life playing as undulating images on that hung white sheet. Her Jewish life in Kolno was nothing like Jewish life in the old-time shtetl in the film. Her life in Kolno was everything like the Jewish life in the old-time shtetl in the film. The story, the bride possessed by the wandering soul of the dead man who had been pledged as her husband, was nothing like her story, was everything like her story. Watching next to her little brother, his skinny body leaning forward, his eyes so intent on the screen it was if they, not the machine next to him, were projecting those flickering illuminations and dark shadows. She remembered how her father would hold a candle next to the faces of people going to America and peer into their eyes, checking for trachoma or other diseases, she knew, but appearing to be staring into their souls. He had held the candle to her face, when they still thought they would immigrate. The story played on the sheet-screen like spreading stains whose vague and suggestive shapes contained constellations of possibilities. Its luminous vision pierced and entered her as had her father's light; she felt like a wandering soul, a dybbuk herself, a stranger that had entered and seized her own body and mind. The film was not her story; it was all her story. Some part of her that was her but larger than her life, as the people on the screen were larger than life, and that somehow made her more real in the world, more real to herself. The old-time shtetl in the film was not Kolno, but the Yiddish, the Hasids, the Magic Rabbi, the familiar Polish landscape, the songs, the songs, the songs, the music, the music, the despised, beautiful desert wailings twisting through dense northern forests and ice, all of it made it hers and continued her on that screen and into the world. That the stories that grew from and into her from the tight, besieged little circle of her world had gone out to the larger world, like the hats she created; that the kind of stories her mother would have told, the stories of her despised people, had gone out to be seen by the strange eyes of goyim, that her despised hybrid of a language was heard by strange ears, shaped into the poetry of the dialogue, somehow magnified and sanctified her as if her life had been blessed by that pure beam of white light playing from the projector, swimming with sparkling motes of dust.

Exactly, Yitzhak says, when she tries to describe it to him and her husband and her brother and her Marxist friends. And her teacher.

Dybbuks, Szapiro whispers, as if in answer to an unspoken question.

Her teacher who had just told them his own story of a taken wife. Why hadn't she thought of that, reined in her untethered tongue? In changing the subject, she had brought them back to the subject. Magnified and sanctified. Had she offended him when she put the words of the mourner's *kaddish* on herself? Stabbed his heart when she described a woman who opened her soul and body up to madness and the dead?

And now you're seeing my Raḥel's wisdom, Rabbi, Elazar says. Her husband, riding in to save her, as he was wont to do. He takes up her hands, kisses both lightly. We only know who we are when we see ourselves reflected in the eyes of other people.

He touches her cheek. Then reaches up and touches Argamaka's face.

Or, he adds, in the eyes of horses.

Her husband.

Chapter Fifteen: The Golem

A rabbi isn't a teacher?

Do you remember that dwarf who taught us, Yitzhak?

Always, Yitzhak says.

What was his name?

Gedalie Ali. Always.

Now that was a pious man, Rabbi.

Light flickers in through the chinks between the weathered planks. A beam falls on the open page of the prayer book and makes the letters swell and shift. Yitzhak, nine years old, watches glowing motes of dust swirl in the beam like something released from the book. His breath tumbles them. He looks back at Gedalie Ali, gesturing energetically at the front of the cheder. As he watches, a beam of sunlight falls on the dwarf also, burning along the edge of his hump so that for an instant Gedalie Ali, in his black gabardine, looks like a cavorting letter, a tiny, twisted Hebrew "gimmel." There had been a rhyme when he'd first learned the alphabet from this same small man. *Gimmel.*

Gamel. The hump of the camel. The light engraves the teacher's lumpy, impish face into the configuration of another, unknown, letter—the dark feathery over-line of the brows, the flared black half-ovals of nostrils, the deep smile grooves around the mouth. The single beam of light thickens the darkness in the rest of the long narrow room; the air is heavy with the dank wet-feather odor of twenty boys sweating in their thick black clothing. They sit transfixed by Gedalie Ali's antics. Squinting, Yitzhak sees the dwarf somehow merging with his own shadow so he grows and becomes hulking, menacing: Esau, the rude and hairy hunter; now, changing—Jacob, besting his violent brother, quick and clever.

Gedalie Ali stops and claps his large gnarled hands, then lets them dangle like oversized gloves from his small, muscular wrists. Yitzhak, at ten, is already taller than his teacher. He loves the dwarf's miniature adultness. When he was five, the Polish woman who had been his wet nurse had given him a tiny carved figure, a crouched evilly-grinning skullish-faced forest imp of great and comical ugliness that he'd loved dearly and carried secretly in his breast pocket until his mother found it and threw it away. The next year, when he had first come to the cheder, he'd thought Gedalie Ali had been fashioned especially for him.

The teacher smiles at him, tugs at a hairy lobe. Recite the passage, *leben*, heart, he says. Slake my ears. The boys giggle. A shiver of love runs through Yitzhak, its quaver passing into the timbre of his voice.

Listen to a Jew, Gedalie Ali admonishes the class. He's panting slightly from his exertions. He puffs up his cheeks and blows out a whoosh of breath, wipes the sweat from his forehead, and turns around to open the window.

Listen to a Jew, Herschel Wolf, the baker's son who sits behind Yitzhak, whispers mockingly in Yitzhak's ear and breaks wind against the wooden bench. Giggles ripple through the room.

Rebbitzin, he whispers, poking Yitzhak in the back, hard. Tiny rabbi's little wifey, he whispers.

Gedalie Ali turns back around slowly and squints into the darkness. Which boil takes it upon itself to burst before I squeeze? he asks sadly. His eyes probe the room, fall on Herschel.

You, baker's get. Dough from the land of dough—rise.

Herschel rises, the pale flesh of his cheeks trembling.

Recite, Gedalie Ali says. Emit something now.

Herschel recites the selection awkwardly, stuttering

and mispronouncing the Hebrew words. The sound of my defeat, Gedalie Ali says, wincing comically, contorting his face so that the boys, even Herschel, laugh. He winks at them, pinches the bridge of his nose and blows delicately. Never mind, child, sit, wait, music will come, even to your life—though you won't hear it if you fart against wood. Now recite, all of you, he says, quickly, sing and drown the misshapen dwarves and halflings this one tries to bring into the world—drown them with the torrent of your words, drown them before they struggle to a monstrous life, I tell you. As the boys laugh and chant raucously, Gedalie Ali listens, one hand behind his ear, his face comically contorted as if in pain.

Reuben Pearle, his eyes worried, appears in the door and gestures to Gedalie Ali. Yitzhak watches the tall horse dealer and the small teacher murmur together, framed by the doorway, the other boys nudging each other at the sight. The sight makes him ache with loss. The last time he'd seen his brother Dov before he'd left for America had been in front of Pearle's horse stalls in the market square, Dov's face pale against a high-collared black Russian shirt that was speckled with spittle from his favorite mare. He'd brought his hand up and stroked her long sad face and the horse nuzzled his hand and whinnied softly, saying her farewell, and Dov had looked at him and nodded without a word, and he'd known it was their farewell also. His brother had grinned at him, the way he did when Yitzhak awakened from a bad dream, as if Dov had been there with him, had ridden in bareback to pull him out of the nightmare.

Keep howling, demons, the teacher tells them. I'll return soon.

But as soon as he leaves, the chanting sputters and stops. Yitzhak finishes the section he is reading silently, so he won't be teased, and brings the pages of the *siddur*, the prayer book, up to his lips. Through the window, he sees Gedalie Ali and Pearle, talking and gesturing, the teacher pacing. *Gimmel, gamel, the hump of the camel.*

Is that his hairy little *tokus*? Herschel taunts, standing up next to him. Yitzhak can feel the other boys stir, their eyes glittering in the dark. He looks back down at the *siddur*.

Herschel draws back his foot and kicks Yitzhak lightly in the shin. Again. Again. Harder. The point of pain grows wider, spreads, burns up his leg. He tries to ignore it and concentrate on the Hebrew lines in front of him. *Baruch ataw adonoy elohanu melach haoloam shay motzay lechem min ha-aretz.* Blessed be you, O Lord our God King of the Universe who has brought bread from the earth. Dough from the land of dough. Yitzhak giggles. Herschel's face twitches and he kicks harder—Don't just sit there, lickspittle, get up and run, run away like your toeless brother. How did he run, lickspittle?

Dov chopped off his toe
because of his nose
But still he goes
Run, golem, run

Herschel recites with no problem now, hovering above Yitzhak, the whole coarse, intruding world gathered into his bloated shape, pressing in, hurting. Yitzhak swings the prayer book at it. A corner of the cover slams into Herschel's forehead, just above his eyes. Herschel's forehead blossoms. Yah, yah, he screams. Yitzhak brings the book back again and starts to swing. A hand grabs his wrist, holds it tightly.

The disappointment in Gedalie Ali's eyes pierces him.

Is this a Jew?

Yitzhak stammers: He said, he called.

He said, he called. And you struck. The world wants our blood and so you draw it for them. As if your brother never left you.

Gedalie Ali takes out his handkerchief, dabs at Herschel's forehead until the bleeding stops. Herschel sobs dramatically. Stop pissing with your eyes, the dwarf says. Enough. He turns to the room. Enough from all of you for now, he says more loudly. Dissolve, clots: go. Nu, what are you waiting for—go. Go, and listen to me now, children, go straight to your houses and go carefully. Don't stray and don't play—this isn't the day for it.

The boys all around Yitzhak rise, buzzing happily at the unexpected holiday. You also, the teacher says to Herschel. Go. Rise, harden, crumble. Live out your cycle. The room empties. Through the open door, Yitzhak can see the grass burning with light, the boys dark whirling specks against the dazzle, tumbling in the weedy yard in front of the *cheder*.

Gedalie Ali goes out and gestures at him to follow. Come, child, I need to chop some wood.

They walk to the side of the building. The wood is stacked against the wall; an ax leans next to the pile.

He said, he called, the teacher repeats finally. And you hit. What did he say to you about your fiery brother?

Nothing, teacher, Yitzhak says.

I've heard his chant before, child. Gedalie Ali shakes his head. Listen and I'll tell you something because you are the brother of your brother, because you have his fire. Because you hit. I'll tell you what he came to understand. The hatred in your heart can become a golem, a monster in the world. A monster that can turn on us and kill us.

The teacher suddenly looks very tired. He presses his fingers to the sides of his head.

Do you understand? No? Listen. Do you know the story of Rabbi Loew, child?

In Prague, Yitzhak mumbles, looking down. He made a cre . . . cre . . . creature.

In Prague he made a cre . . . cre . . . creature, Gedalie Ali says. In Prague when the Jews were threatened and killed as we are in this world, Rabbi Loew took clay and fashioned it over the bones of the martyred dead into the shape of a huge man, and with his own fingers, like this—Gedalie Ali writes in the air—can you see him, Yitzhak? the teacher says, his eyes shadowed under his thick, tangled eyebrows, the jutting bones of his forehead echoing, strangely, the ridge of hump on his bowed little back—can you see how with his fingers, their tips burning with anger, he wrote the word *emet*, truth, in the clay of the creature's forehead and he breathed the heat of his heart into the clay mouth and then life pushed veins under the clay. That night the golem rose, and that night and every night it went out into the streets of

Prague and killed the killers of the Jews, broke their bones, sealed off the breath in their throats. Until one day it killed without the rabbi telling it to, and the rabbi was afraid that he could no longer control the creature, that the living clay would harm the innocent. That it would bring the vengeance of the gentiles down on our heads. He understood, you see, that we survive by moving between the raindrops, child, by the magic of invisibility and weightlessness. Do you know what he did then? No? It was simple, child. Gedalie Ali squats and draws the word *emet,* truth, in the dust with his finger. He turned truth into death. So. The dwarf rubs away the *aleph*, leaves *met*, death in the dust. Truth into death. That simple. He destroyed the creature he'd created to be our protector and avenger. But it was necessary. It was simply necessary. There was nothing else to do. The creature had to go.

Run, golem, run.

Gedalie Ali squints at him. Do you understand my story, child? No? Never mind; your brother did—that's what's important. It's all right. I'll put the words here, later they'll hatch.

The spatulate forefinger moves to Yitzhak's forehead, its warmth pulsing into his head.

Go now, child; I'm tired and you drink me like a cup.

He picks up the ax and turns his back on Yitzhak. The ax is nearly his size but he handles it as if it is light as a matchstick. Yitzhak stares at the hands wrapped around the haft, the reddened knuckles misshapen and bulbous, the muscle cords under the arm fur twitching and sliding. The bobbing hump on the dwarf's back seems suddenly to hold another, evil brain, driving the powerful arms with maniacal fury. Gedalie Ali raises the ax over the white ax wedge of his face, his expression fierce under his bristling, coarse eyebrows, a changeling hatched into the world. *Gimmel, gamel, golem.*

It begins to rain. Yitzhak watches a light wedge-shaped slash in a log soak and darken. Gedalie Ali's words merge into the words he'd heard between Dov and his father the night before Dov left, the murmur of their voices awakening him. He'd crept to the landing, the way he always did, and he could see the two of them in Papa's room, his brother standing near the large horsehair chair. He'd felt a flutter of fear—only travelers came to that chair: Papa would light a candle, hold it to their faces and peer into their eyes as if to see something inside their heads, a *trachoma*, a quality they must have if they would pass to America. He'd listened to them, straining to understand the mysterious prayer-language of adults, the sing-song of passages and commentaries whose meanings danced like motes of dust just outside his understanding, yet sifted into his memory so he could recite, word for word, as he would *Gemara*, a dialogue of rabbis:

And Dov said: What do you expect to see if you look into my eyes with your light, papa?

And Papa said: Your soul.

And Dov said: How mystical—I thought you searched only for trachoma.

And Papa said: The eye is like an egg; when I put light to it, I see the soul curled inside its cavity. I see it uncurl and move along paths of possibility. Why do you smile?

And Dov said: I see why they pay you. How does it look, papa? The soul?

And Papa said: How do you think? A soft, red, transluctantly luminous sac, as fine-veined as the fetus I once saw ripped from the belly of a Jewish girl by a drunken Russian. Sit.

And Dov sat, his back stiff, his hands gripping the armrests.

And Papa lit the candle and seized Dov's wrist and brought the candle closer with his other hand.

And Dov said: So, nu, can my eyes stand the light of America?—are they focused enough so all they'd see would be dollars? You're the one who should go—the Jews' benches in that land are only for the Negroes. You could have gone to university, been a physician there, instead of a smuggler. Instead of a dealer in trachoma certificates for would-be travelers.

And Papa said: If the queen had balls. If Jews were gentiles. But we're not, are we?

And Dov said: We can only try.

And Papa said: Is that what you're doing?

And Dov said: What exactly do you see in my eyes, Papa.

And Papa said: A dark flow. Blood and flames. Something loosening and releasing terrible things upon us.

And Dov said: What's loose is already loose in the world. So you know. Is that why you have me in this chair? Is that why you want me to leave? In Vilna last week, gentiles melted the candelabra of the synagogue and poured it down the rabbi's throat, saying he was known for his silver tongue. Polish wit. You tell me about a Russian birth; I tell you about a Polish insemination. If you wish, I have more stories.

And Papa said: A terrible story doesn't free you to do terrible things.

And Dov said: It gives them the license of example to exist. It loosens them into life.

And Papa stared into Dov's eyes and said: Like a golem?

And Dov said: So you know that too.

And Papa said: I'm not alone in that knowledge. Golem . . . how mystical. I thought your organization searched only for earthly solutions.

And Dov said: We regard it as an accurate metaphor. The golem was a construct, a creature of the anger in our hearts, an instrument of terror against those who terrorized us. Terror against terror.

And Papa said: Examine that metaphor. Once loosened, the golem couldn't be bridled. The creator became the creature of his creature.

And Dov looked down and said: The golem was a limited strategic action. A means to an end. When its goal was met, it was discontinued. Just like that. And if it gets out of control, so what? The task of terror is to set chaos into motion, to let a terrible situation spin out of control. In other words, what do we lose? Lives? Lives will be lost anyway, one way or another.

And Papa said: Whose words are you reciting to convince yourself? You know what will be lost, heart. I can see into you. Your eyes blink and I'm taken and carried by a dream that blows into my head like a dark wind. Darkness moving softly into darkness.

And for a moment Dov said nothing. And closed his eyes.

And said: Are you worried about my soul or everybody else's ass?

And said: I have a new wife with a child in her womb.

And Papa said: Sarah will stay with her parents in Lomza until you can send for her; I've spoken to them.

And Dov said: Papa, I don't know what to do. I cut off my toes so I wouldn't have to kill. So I could stay here. Now I have to sever myself from myself.

And Papa said: Hazak hazak v'nit hazak. *Strength and more strength.*

Gedalie Ali's ax swings down. Yitzhak sees his brother holding his bare foot against a stump, his face intent, the identical arc, the toes flying like bullets. *I liberated them from my foot, little one, in order to liberate myself.* He'd freed himself, but now he'd had to run anyway, run without toes.

Papa brought the flame closer.

Run golem run.

What would his father see if he looked into his eyes? What did the dwarf see? Yitzhak suddenly knows the truth, *emet*, written on his own forehead, knows what Gedalie Ali had been trying to tell him, knows he's his brother's brother, understands the passage now, knows what he has to do. He closes his eyes. The candle flame still flickers behind his lids. He stares at the small bright twist, the little skullish face at its blue center, the candlelight licking its dark sockets. The face swells out of the light, rises to his kiss: clay flesh cracked to expose white skullbone, black Hebrew letters gouged into the forehead, clawed down around the deep blood-welled eye sockets, the curved grin of broken teeth outlined and stained with red mud, the forehead engraved with truth, *emet*, the letter *aleph*, he must erase to create death, to kill the killer in his heart.

Now I have to sever myself from myself.

Hazak v'et hazak.

The ax rises, begins to fall. He rushes forward, brushes by Gedalie Ali's legs, sticks his hand, the hand that struck at Herschel, the golem's hand, onto the wet wood altar waiting under the fall of the arc. A part of him that sees the way his soul sees the dream now sees the dwarf twisting the ax desperately, the sharp edge turning away, up, but the arc completes itself, down, a bone-grinding grip seizes and thrusts his hand into the candle flame and it sears up through his veins and bursts behind his eyes and he stretches and flickers long and thin and impossibly thin and out.

And comes back, slowly. A drifting dust of letters gathering on an empty page. Lying in a thick silence. In blackness. In rain. In mud. He hears the sound of his own breathing in it and he knows he has breath. He hears breathing over him and a warm spot of breath touches his face and he knows he has flesh. The pain pulses in his hand like a heart, and he knows he has flesh.

He feels himself gripped, pulled up embraced against a hard, warm chest.

He opens his eyes and sees Gedalie Ali's stricken face, his hairy cheeks streaked with mud or blood or rain or tears. I know, I know, the dwarf is saying, rocking him. Shah, it's all right, my light, I know, and Yitzhak feels his teacher gently writing the letters that will bring him to life or death on the cool smoothness of his forehead.

Chapter Sixteen: Bread and Salt

Let them come, she had said to Elazar when they'd spoken in the past about the possibility of a German invasion. Better the civilized Germans than the savage Russians, with their pogroms, Cossacks and Commissars. He had not argued, just quietly said: you don't know them. It was true, she had heard stories of what the Germans were doing to Jews; she'd seen the burning synagogue and the hateful mob framed by a boxcar door as if contained safely in a painting or film. But most of their relatives and neighbors discounted the worst tales. They knew the Germans; they lived across a porous border from them, worked with them, traded with them. The nation of Bach and Beethoven, of Heine, Goethe, and Einstein would not descend into the barbarity of the Cossacks and Slavs.

Her husband had not been in Kolno when the Germans came to the town. When they finally invaded in September, he had put on his old uniform and went to reenlist in the army. And was accepted, in spite of his age and her prayers. He and a contingent from Kolno had made it to Warsaw, in time to be bombed by the Luftwaffe and to witness the Polish surrender. In October the Germans poured south, out of that fragile border with Prussia, and quickly taken Kolno and Lomza. Elazar, his army unit disbanded, had made it to the Piska forest and for a time joined with the local Polish resistance under Stanislaw Milewski, but he left and hid in the forest when some of his comrades tried to kill him for being a Jew.

Raḥel had watched as many of her Polish neighbors welcomed the Germans, handing the traditional bread and salt up to dust-covered soldiers sitting in the backs of trucks. The soldiers looked young to her, nodding off to sleep even as their vehicles lumbered down Lomza Street. One soldier, who looked even younger than her brother Yitzhak, took off his goggles, leaving two startlingly white circles, like a mask, around his blue eyes, startling against the black dusted skin of his cheeks, lips, and chin. He looked to Raḥel like one of the cartoon characters she had seen in the Alhambra.

The Endeks hung a Swastika flag on the town hall. Some of the Poles lining the street as the Germans rolled in cheered and applauded. Once the trucks passed, they began breaking into Jewish homes. They dragged out the Levinsky family, stabbing Ida the seamstress and her husband Yakub in front of Grisha, their 12-year-old son. Mika, a farmer from near Zabiele, strangled the boy. He and his brothers drove a cart up to the house and loaded it up with the Levinsky's clothing and furniture and, Raḥel was sure, jewelry, stepping over the corpses on their way in or out. That night, four other homes were looted and burned.

Raḥel and Sarah Gittel hear about the Levinsky's from Wanda, who came knocking on their locked door. Where is your boxer when we need him, Sarah Gittel asks.

Fighting these beasts.

These beasts? The Germans just open a gate the Poles press against. These are our own beasts devouring us. Come.

Raḥel stares at her. Come where?

Sarah Gittel is putting on her coat.

Your gangster is not here. Your brother is hiding. Your papa is dead. Your other brother and sisters sit in America like little princes and princesses. Come. There is only us. We must stop this. It is unseemly. Come.

Where?

To church.

Ema, take off your coat. You're insane.

Come. Or stay.

She steps out of the door.

Who is this woman, Raḥel thinks.

As they walk towards the Catholic church, Raḥel sees one of her Christian friends, Halina Golshovska, gesturing at her frantically from her doorway. When Raḥel draws closer, Halina pulls her inside.

Pani Brikman, please come in too, she pleaded.

I go to the priest, Sarah Gittel says, in her broken Polish.

For a minute, please, come inside.

When the two women have entered, they see the Polish woman is sobbing. Halina, speak to me, Raḥel says.

That pig Wlodkowski and some farmers. I saw them kill the Mayzler girls.

Chana and Miriam, Sarah Gittel asks sharply.

They stripped them naked, in the street, made them walk in front of them. Halina looks into Raḥel's eyes, her stare suddenly fierce. Miriam was wonderful. It's the only word. She refused to cover herself or cower. She held her head high, told them to get the eyeful they could only dream about. Look, she told them, enjoy, tomorrow your cocks will drop off. She cursed them as they raped her, as they killed her. And her sister. Virgin girls.

I go, Sarah Gittel says to Raḥel. You stay.

Please, Pani Brikman. Stay here, Halina said. My husband and I can hide you in the cellar.

I go.

Who is this woman?

I'm going with you, Halina says.

As they walk to the church, the streets are deserted, silent. But they hear the crackle of fire, shouts from the other side of town.

The priest, Father Alexandroski, is lighting candles as they enter. Inside, under the high arch of the ceiling, it was cool and dark and silent, filled with shadows. The candlelight reflects off gold and silver candlesticks and the vestaments of the priest. The crucified Christ stares down at Raḥel. Neither she nor her mother have ever set foot inside this building. She hunches her shoulders as if a cold wind is blowing on her.

You should not be here, the priest says, as if reading words written on Raḥel's mind. She is about to say something, agree, but again her mother, her new mother, the woman who had grown her hair secretly and flung away her wig, was the one who speaks.

Your people, she says. You must stop. They kill. They . . . She hesitated, searching for the Polish word.

Rape, Raḥel and Halina say, almost at once.

Your people reap the whirlwind, the priest said.

The wind?

They are communists. Communists and Christ-killers.

And the children, are they communists, Father, Halina asks. She was trembling with anger.

There is nothing I can do. Leave.

Raḥel wants to. The walls of this place are squeezing in on her, the smell of the incense is nauseating. Christ-killer. She recalls Elazar telling her they called him that in the army, the same army he had gone to now. She sees her mother stare at the priest and nod, as if something has been confirmed.

The old priest would have helped. Come away from here, she says to the two other women.

Shall we go home or to Halina's, Raḥel asks her. We need to find Yitzhak.

Come.

On Gromazin Street Sarah Gittel knocks on the door of the Dulovich bakery. When no one answers, she twisted the knob; the door swung open. Raḥel understands: Lev Dulovich knew if the mob came, they would break down the door anyway; tried this way to save having to make repairs. There is a kind of hope in that gesture that saddens rather than soothes her, speaking as it does to the kind of soothes knowledge Dulovich carried.

Her mother calls out the baker's name. Silence. Sarah Gittel sighs, goes behind the counter and brings out four challehs and a loaf of black rye. Her mother has gone insane. *Ema*, she says gently.

Come, Sarah Gittel says again. Or stay.

Outside they hear more shouts and screams, the sound of breaking glass. They follow Sarah Gittel until they saw she is moving towards the town hall. The German trucks are parked outside; the red, white, and black swastika banner hanging over the door.

Are you insane, Ema? Stop.

Come or stay, *pickholtz.* I know them, all my life. They are refined people.

Raḥel thinks of physically restraining her mother. As if sensing it, Sarah Gittel cuts in front of her and shuffles quickly up the steps. Some of the German soldiers look at them, one saying something to another, a fattish boy with black hair and an echoing black mole on his cheek. The boy laughs.

Halina, go home, Raḥel says. There is no reason to let Halina be destroyed by her mother's insanity.

Look, Halina says.

Sarah Gittel has been met at the top of the steps by an older German with, what Raḥel takes to be, an officer's insignia on the collar of his gray uniform. The uniform is as filthy as those of the other soldiers; the man's beard-stubbled face even more tired. He is staring at Sarah Gittel with an expression of disbelief. As Raḥel rushes up the steps, she fights the urge to bring her hand up to cover the back of her neck, or to turn around: the cords of her neck are tense with the anticipation of a bullet. Another German has come up next to the first, younger but with the same air of command. She hears a few words spill from Sarah Gittel's mouth, fears hearing her mother telling these Germans to go shit in the ocean. We no harm, good people. Good German friends, many years, she hears Sarah Gittel say in her broken German. To Raḥel's shock, the older officer looks amused.

Look, Madame, he says. We're just field soldiers. It's none of our business.

Sarah Gittel pushes the bread at him. You help. Hooligans. *Goniffs*.

He takes the bread from her, cradling it in his arms, bringing it like a bouquet to his nose. Suddenly he chuckles.

The younger officer looks alarmed. No, Alfred, you can't get . . .

Fuck them, the older man says.

He turns to Sarah Gittel. I'll send some men out. It will be quiet tonight.

Who is this woman?

Sarah Gittel says nothing as they walk back to the house.

It was quiet that night, the only noise a burst of machine gun fire over the heads of some of the Poles gathering with clubs, hoes, and axes near the market square. They disperse, running away down different streets.

The next day, the Germans pile back into their trucks and leave.

The streets remain empty. To Raḥel the town seemed an exhausted soldier itself, energy-less and passive, panting out its tired breaths.

On the Sabbath, another German unit roared into town: five motorcycles with sidecars, a number of open-backed lorries. These Germans wore black uniforms with silver skulls on their collars, and were clean-shaven and spotless, their boots shined. *Einsatzgruppe V*, Halina said, indentifying them later to Raḥel. Whatever that means. They did not look tired. Some of the Poles, including many of the Endecja men started coming out onto the streets again. As if they had been signaled. The Germans smiled and nodded at the waving Poles. They parked in front of the town hall—no one had removed the swastika flag. The men jumped down from the first lorry and one of them shot Shmuel Radowicz who was standing and watching, and another his wife Chana, who ran towards them screaming as her husband fell. Raḥel, telling this later to Elazar, supposed that Shmuel, with his *payot*, long black caftan and full black beard, *Tzitzit* fringes dangling below his vest, looked like the Eternal Jew Himself.

Now you'll see, Yids, Dombrovski the Endek had screamed.

All that day the motorcyclists buzzed through town, with the soldiers in the side-cars announcing through electronic megaphones that all citizens of Kolno who were not kikes or collaborators should gather at the movie theater. Led to it by Dombrovski and the other Endeks, the readers of Heine and Goethe kicked open the doors to the Alhambra. They had brought their own projector and screen. Where Raḥel watched *The Dybbuk*, they showed *The Eternal Jew* to the Christian citizens of Kolno, as recounted by Maja and Wanda. Such an evil demon, that Jew, Maja had said, spitting onto the floor. Many people in the audience, she also said, were not from town, but from the farms. At the end of the show, Shiviatlovski, the police commander, an Endek, had led a mob that broke into Jewish homes and slaughtered whoever they found. Over thirty people, Raḥel believed, though she had not been sure of the count. She knew from Wanda that the Germans had shot ten young Poles who had refused to participate in the killing of Jews. She was certain they raped and killed her friend, Chava Beylkeh, in front of her son, Szymon, and then they killed him. She was certain they brought carts to each of the houses they broke into, and loaded up with furniture and whatever valuables they could find. She didn't know why their house was spared that night. There was no logic to it, only the insane randomness of a storm,

Elazar was not there to witness the pogrom. He was not there to witness Argamaka taken by Yankayitis. He was not there to witness how she tried to trample him to death. He was not there when the school master, limping painfully with a shattered right hip, gave her to the Germans as a gift, nor, after she had broken the jaw of a sergeant with a blow from her right rear hoof, the German had shot both Argamaka and Yankayitis to death.

He was there though, sneaking into Kolno from the forest, in time to witness the visit of Reichsmarschall Herman Goring to their town, an occasion celebrated in the

Reichsmarschall's honor by the murder of forty more Jews by the soldiers of Einsatzgruppe V, helped by the usual Endeks.

He is here now, in time to witness the withdrawal of the Germans on the 29th of September under the Ribbentrop-Molotov Pact when the town and half of Poland is put back into Mother Russia's arms again.

He is here to witness the Endeks Dombrovski, Wlodkowski, and Shiviatlovski, the police chief thrown back in jail by the Soviets.

He is here to witness as many of the Jews of Kolno, including his brother-in-law Yitzhak and cousins by marriage Beryl and Rivka, hand the traditional bread and salt to the Russian soldiers as they march into town down Lomza Street.

Chapter Seventeen: Lenin Comes to Kolno

When Raḥel, accompanied by Sarah Gittel, comes back to her father's grave, it is to secure his blessing on the child she carries in her womb.

The stones she left during her last visit are still here but the world has become molten, flowing into new channels cut from fire. She and her mother stand as motionless as a picture, a portrait they would have taken with them if they had gone to America and could never again gather at this grave. Neither woman weeps. They are sepia images on paper, as blank of feeling as they are drained of color. Ghosts.

A breeze rustles through the leaves of the white birch trees that crest the little hillock behind the grave; it sways and bobs the heads of the purple poppies carpeting the earth. Papa, borders disperse like mist, like dreams. Kolno is again in Russia as it had been when she was a young girl, whether it was called the Soviet Union or the Land of the Munchkins, another story she had seen on Yitzhak's sheet-screen. Germany has gobbled half of Poland; Russia devoured the rest. Once again the world has moved under her feet as she stood still. Papa we are here. We can't smuggle ourselves out like swaths of fine damask or beautiful horses. Borders change like dreams but we are stuck as stones in the earth. Too late. We didn't go to America, with my brothers and sisters. We didn't go to France, like cousin Aaron. Or to Palestine like cousin Bruria. Or to Argentina, like cousins Haim, Moshe, and Zelig Lobel.

Or to Russia, she thinks, with her brother Yitzhak and her cousins Beryl and Rivka, all three arrested by the Communists for not being Communist enough, and sent to labor camps in Siberia or the Urals. Swept up like the dust of history. Or was it into the dust-bin of history? Raḥel remembers Rivka using one term or another; remembers the couple's lazy, good-humored arguments with her and Elazar and the *melamed* Chaim Szapiro. Drinking slivovitz, smoking thin black cigarettes, watching the other young people strolling through the market square, buying from the stalls, talking passionately, self-conscious of how modern they looked. Arguing over films. Arguing with fascists. Such moments seem luxurious now; she longs for mundane trivialities.

Some of the Jewish Koloners, mostly communists, had fled voluntarily into Russia proper, fear of the Germans returning driving them farther east. More townspeople, both Jews and Poles, had simply been arrested or deported to the Soviet Union, though many Endeks, including Basil Dombrovski had been thrown in the Kolno jail. Making those Poles, who anyway saw all Jews as communists, hate them even more. No one knew the fate of all those taken to Russia. They were gone. Her cousins and brother were gone. She and Elazar and Sarah Gittel were here.

That any of us is here is a miracle, Papa.

Beryl's shed had been taken down even before Beryl was taken, along with all the other sheds and stalls and shops in and around the market square. The shops had been closed; the stalls burned, leaving a checkerboard of black squares on the ground in front of their house. At its center, a statue of Lenin now stood, carted in one night so that he was there frowning at them when they woke at dawn. Listen, Baldy, how could you call a blacksmith an unproductive element, she wanted to ask him when she first saw the statue. How was a seller of schmattes a capitalist exploiter, your stony honor? Did horses no longer need to be shod, humans no longer need to be clothed, you gloomy, fox-bearded son of a bitch? A black cholera on you. And what of the delight of hats, those crowns for women? And what about the eye that peered into the light and saw the soul on a screen made from the sheet of a bridal bed? These questions on more minds than hers, but never finished their journey to anyone's lips. Everyone knew the answer would be barked out in the language of clubs or bullets.

Too late, Papa.

And now Jews have a new trade anyway, pressed into labor *antels* to dig defensive trenches around the town. Her husband, who still possessed the constitution and brawn of a boxer, would drag himself home after dark, leaning on her, both of them covered with dirt, muddied with sweat, reeling as if dizzied by blows. His opponent not only the hard red Polish earth that mocked and resisted their pickaxing and shoveling as it always had their presence, not only the commissars who had taken away their livelihoods and worked and beat them like the Pharaoh's taskmasters, but also an egg-like lump that had developed in his groin and thigh and that was making his leg swell painfully, so by the end of the day he was dragging it after him as if fettered to a heated iron chain. In the evening she sees the boxer, the fighter he once was, standing in one of the black squares skipping rope as he had done in countless gymnasiums, in Bialystok, in Warsaw, in Minsk and Kyiv, but now grunting in pain each time his right foot struck the ground. Why, she had asked him, but she knew why.

At night she pressed a cold cloth to the lump. He would wince in pain. Sometimes the press would arouse him and she would move her hand over to caress him. She needed him but she had seen him shudder in agony when he entered her, as if he were the virgin being penetrated, and she had come to feel that painful act of love was joined to what skipping rope, his boxer's exercise, was to him: a way to prove he was still whole, still a man. To prove to her, to prove to himself.

To finally be with child now, with the arrival of the Germans and then the Russians, with the revolt of her husband's own body, seems a cruel mockery.

She puts her hand on top of her father's cold headstone, prays for her husband, for herself, for her mother, for the child in her womb, all of them. The birch trees on the hillock sway and their leaves flutter up, flashing silver. The blue poppies whisper and bend and bow and straighten and bow again, a brilliant congregation, their beauty insane. Beyond the trees the river boils black. She knows she should not pray to a human being, but to *HaShem.* She knows she should not be praying at her father's grave for someone to stick a jagged stone up that statue's Russian *tokus*.

She is exhausted and hungry. She misses the hat factory, her workbench and designs. All childless women have also been drafted into the *antels*; she keeps her pregnancy a secret so she can stay with Elazar, pays for it when she drags herself back after sunset with the child a boulder in her gut and her limping husband refusing to put more weight on her. Were not men and women equal in the New Paradise, Baldy? All day she dug, sometimes with a shovel, sometimes with her bare hands, broken, calloused and claw-like, reaching into and bringing that Polish soil to her, to all of them, as if it were finally taking them under its skin.

Why are they digging what they are digging, are the questions the Jews ask themselves, the new *pilpul,* the central query of their new Talmudic debate. The Germans and the Russians have divided Poland as if the child dumped before King Solomon had actually been cut in two to satisfy both mothers. But if that mutilation had brought peace, why were they digging what they had heard the Russians call anti-tank ditches to the west of Kolno, along the roads to Meschtshevoye and Kolimagi? To the west, from which the Germans would come, if they returned.

Her brothers and sisters have gotten out, but she and her husband and her mother, who sits at home muttering to herself, are going nowhere. Hunger, uncertainty, inertia, her mother's bitter presence, Elazar's rotting leg and the baby growing in her womb all anchor them. Perhaps if the Germans came back, it would be no worse than these Communists. After all, the German commander her mother had confronted was a human being. They—the Jews of Kolno; they, the Brikman family, would suffer what would befall them like their ancestors had suffered the Inquisition, the ghettos, the expulsions. They would suffer and endure it as they had suffered and endured the blood libels the massacres and the pogroms; some would be broken, many would die, but eventually the enemy would be destroyed or leave or die thwarted and bewildered and scratching themselves and the survivors would emerge from cellars and hiding places as if from the grave and begin again. Create a new holiday to celebrate another survival. To thank Ha-Shem for putting his chosen ones into the fire in order to save them again, teach them something or other. *Am Yisrael Chai.* The People Israel Live. Mostly.

Isn't that so, Papa?

Chapter Eighteen: Altar

Years before, Raḥel's father, dreaming, sees his other sons and daughters standing on a verdant shore, gesturing to him: leave, flee west, find a ship, put an ocean between you and this place where we were unwanted guests. Their mouths are open and he can hear them scream. The scream forms a silver knife in Pinhas's dream, cuts a cord in him, and he tumbles awake. As if his mind is still caught in the motion of his dream, he rolls out of bed and pulls on his clothing and his boots. Sitting on the edge of the bed, he is no longer sure if the scream was real. He thinks he should get up and check but is reluctant to face another crisis. If he goes back to sleep, perhaps it will dissolve. He rubs his face. His wife, Sarah Gittel, sleeps uneasily, muttering, her face, nested on the blood-stained feathers spilling from the ripped pillows, twisted into an expression of bitter triumph. Perhaps the noise was from a wild animal. Foxes and boars were coming out of the forest at night now, into the ruined streets of the town, sometimes even wolves, more of these now; they were developing a preference for human flesh. He has heard people have been attacked but doesn't believe it likely:

the wolves could find enough fresh human carrion without having to endanger themselves. Watching the bloody feathers stirring under his wife's breath, he remembers the stories his father had told him when he was a child about Chmielnicki, the Cossack Hetman, and his massacre of the seven hundred Jewish communities. His father had spoken of these things with a kind of strange tenderness, a comforting tone, as if to reassure him that the days when men were beasts had safely passed into stories.

The scream pierces the air again. This time Sarah Gittel sits up, her cry echoing and trailing out the howl from downstairs.

Be calm—he's probably only having a bad dream, Pinhas says. He gets up and goes out through the salon, wincing at the bullet-torn, ax-splintered wreckage of their furniture: the samovar his grandfather had given him dented into junk, the upholstered sofa he'd transported from Danzig slashed, stuffing hanging out of its wounds, the Belgian carpet covered with mud and blood stains, the gutted clock. Wallpaper, damaged by the rain and snow coming in through the broken windows, hangs in soggy, fleshy strips from the walls. Sarah Gittel has not allowed him to clean any of this wreckage.

He walks into the children's room. Raḥel is standing

over her brother's bed, patting his head with a damp cloth. He smiles to see her.

Raḥel, he says. Let me look.

He lights a candle next to the bed. Yitzhak moans as Pinhas picks up his hand, Pinhas noticing, not letting his daughter see him notice, the amount of blood that has dripped on the floor and bedding. When Yitzhak was wounded last month, he had treated the injury himself, afraid to go to the Polish clinic. The world is insane, the way we live in it, his other son Dov had said. That's neither here nor there, Pinhas said. *Nichstihier, nichstihein.* Now the wounded hand lies palm up on the sheet, gushing blood into a pattern, writing an accusation. He leans closer and sniffs. The blood smells bad. Get clean linen, more water, he says to his mother. Boil the water.

Papa, there's no wood.

Smash something. Use the clock. Do what you can, child.

His son must have torn out the stitching he'd done. The thumb is mashed and nearly off, not healing. The small torn tab of flesh tears at his heart: its vulnerability taking his mind to the quick dart of the mohel's knife at Yitzhak's circumcision, the answering tingle in his own flesh, a connection of his maleness to his son's, the wounds that bind them to a covenant of cuts and lost pieces. He thinks of his son Dov who had cut off two toes to escape from being pulled into the army. From which army was this boy escaping? His wife and daughter come into the room. Sarah Gittel draws in her breath sharply.

Murderer, she says.

For an instant he sees how he must look to her, tall and bearded in moon and candlelight, hovering over the broken form of his son.

Just help me. Later reproach me for my life.

She is holding the last of the Shabbat candles in one hand, linen samples he'd smuggled before the fighting in the other. Raḥel comes in with a bowl of water. He washes the wound again, Yitzhak moaning in fever and pain. Sarah Gittel picks up the hand and holds it while he rewraps it.

I must get him to a doctor. The blood may be poisoned.

I thought you were doctor enough, Sarah Gittel says. Doctor smuggler—you should have smuggled us away. What will you do now: make a doctor out of a column of snow, breathe life into its nostrils?

Hoffman's on the other side of the border.

On the other side of the moon.

He finishes wrapping the bandage. For a few

seconds, the thumb is hidden by the white, pure linen. But, as he watches, a spreading spot of red brings out the pattern of the weave. He starts to unwrap the wound.

Get your needle and thread.

Cholera, Sara Gittel curses.

She leaves the room. In a few moments she comes back with the wooden box in which she keeps her sewing things. She holds up a needle to the candlelight and threads it, squinting, ties it off, then looks impatiently at her daughter.

What are you studying me to learn? Go to the kitchen and bring the bottle of vodka your father hides there. I've shown you where it is.

When she comes back, Pinhas uncorks the bottle and takes a drink in front of his wife's eyes, then pours the vodka over Yitzhak's hand. The boy screams. Pinhas sees a pure white spur of bone in the center of the wound, before the blood wells in again.

Pour, scoundrel, Sarah Gittel says. You'll get more.

He pours. Hold his wrist, he tells her. She holds it tightly, staring into his eyes. But when he brings the tip of the needle to his son's skin, his hand trembles. Without a word of reproach, Sarah Gittel takes the needle from his fingers. He pours, she sews. Her hand doesn't tremble. He feels a surge of love for her, then hate, each quickening his blood in the same way.

Strapped chest and shoulders to the sled, he pulls his son through the Piska forest. The runners break heavily through the crust and resist his pull; he's wrapped the boy with thick horse blankets over swaths of fine linen he smuggled from Danzig through this same forest. The wind twirls sparkling columns of snow up between the birch and pine trees; when he breathes deeply the icy air scratches his lungs. His breath, sparkling, dances like delirium in front of his eyes.

Loud cracks boom from deep in the forest, trees exploding in the cold. Smuggler's weather.

Five versts, he thinks. To go on the road is impossible in any case. Bands of deserters are murdering travelers for food, clothing, the brief fricative warmth of rape. He knows where to go: this is the white crack between countries in which he moves. The snow mist swirls and wraps around his legs and up his body, veils the trunks of the trees so they seem transparent, ghosts of trees. He the consciousness in that swirling mist, its brittling breath, *Ruah*. The cold edges into the warmth of his lungs, a nuzzle of death. When he looks back he can't see the sled, only the rope he is attached to disappearing into blinding white.

He pulls against the weight, fighting its soft sinking into the snow. Beads of sweat form on his face, freeze and fall tinkling. The burning coldness he gasps into his lungs moves to his stomach, his heart: he feels his bones growing thin and brittle. Bird bones. He bends forward and draws harder and he is light and hollow boned as a bird and he lets the lightness flow back and hollow the rope, pass into the sled and its burden and he rises with it now in the swirling white cloud, into the sky, up and up until he is above the mist and can see it below, the black spear tops of the firs sticking out of its milky thickness and now the whole forest stretching below him, the church spire of the town, the market square teeming with men and women and animals embracing and bowing and jumping up and down in a strange dance, a pattern which only could be seen from above. He soars, carried up in a draft that pushes his chest and stomach like someone pressing a pillow up against him and at the top of his gyre he can see everything, the Prussian border to the north and west, the Russian border to the north and east of the Pale, locked together like teeth; he flows in between, a human being smuggling his own human heart. He sees the cracks between nations swarming with dark bearded men, smugglers with glittering eyes, the gleaming, sea-salt crusted city of Danzig, the twisting streets and narrow alleys of Bialystok, the red domes of Moscow; if he soars higher he will see Jerusalem itself, a tawny city straddling mountains like a sleeping lion.

A tree, its black trunk glazed bright with ice, appears before him, spears him back to the earth. He pulls his frozen eyelids apart. In the slit he watches the tree bulge, the ice swelling in its veins. The tree splits with a loud crack as if sundered by an invisible ax; its insides show white as a bone in a wound. Who has ever seen such a sight? He kneels and picks up a heavy branch split from the exploded tree, to help him walk, to weigh him to earth. What a strange land I've been made a stranger in and must move in with this weight. Will You speak to me now with wonders and miracles from this tree that doesn't burn? What will You ask of me now for there's no mountain here and no altar and no ram to give in my son's place but You can't have him, this one, I'll walk on this earth with this one. You have enough of my children.

The whirling snow parts like a curtain and reveals a dim hulked shape fast against the base of a birch tree. Fear squeezes his heart but he moves closer. A tapered, gentle brown face forms, fur beaded with balls of ice, soft brown eyes open under cataracts of ice, spikes of ice hanging from the antlers, the stag leaning stiff against the tree, knees locked. *Tzaar baal hayim*, pity for living things.

Nevertheless, it is a miracle; he'd asked for a ram and had been given this, a life given instead of a life. He brings his face close, his breath stirring the fur, and stares into the animal's eyes. A flicker of warmth blinks into him, a hot corner of its soul.

Stop, a voice says.

He stares wildly at the deer, his heart beating.

Here, you bastard.

Here another miracle, a bear waiting against an oak next to the birch, its black matted brows and hairy face thick with ice, breath steaming from its red nostrils and lips. Pinhas comes closer, gripping the icy stick in his numb hand. The bear becomes a man, a deserter, or a wounded soldier left to freeze, sitting with one hand casually in his lap; the man growls at him. The man's right leg is outstretched in front of him at an odd angle from his body, the snow around it spotted red.

Come, brother, whoever you are, help me.

Sir, my son is hurt. I'm taking him to a doctor.

The man laughs, coughs like a bear. Where's his hospital—in a tree? Is he a bird? He peers brightly at Pinhas. *Zhid*, ain't it? What are you doing here, with your little *zhid* son? Is he on the sled? *Farshivy zhid*, he's dead by now, in this cold.

No.

The man laughs. He moves his hand, revealing a pistol in his other hand. Come closer, come on, bring the sled. Hurry up—no stalling. I'm starving and freezing, you son of a bitch.

The man has turned back into a bear. Pinhas, on the other hand, turns into a *farshivy zhid.* Fawning, craven. Harmless. The bear laughs with satisfaction. I asked for a ram, but a bear will do, Pinhas thinks as he swings the stick heavily against the matted jaw. The eyes widen and the mouth drops open in astonishment. He hits the head again and then again, the hardness of the skull giving and then softening. A cell of death moves up the icy stick and into his hand and arm.

He flips the body over, puts the gun in his coat pocket and strips off the fur coat and gloves. He brings them back to the sled and covers Yitzhak. Holding his breath, he uncovers Yitzhak's face. He puts his lips on his son's lips. Ice to ice. He stays, fastened, breathing into the boy until he feels a spot of warmth on his lips and closes his eyes and drinks his son's breath, its warmth moving through his body, flowing everywhere except into the arm and hand that had gripped the stick. They remain heavy as if full of ice. He takes off his other glove and grasps his skin there. It feels as if he's pinching the flesh of a stranger. He nods, understanding, a death instead of a death, another piece of himself clipped in exchange for a covenant. He begins moving again through the forest, earth bound, gripping the strap around his chest with his left hand, his right arm useless, dead as a frozen branch.

Chapter Nineteen: Dandelions

A July thunderstorm, she thinks, as the flash blinds her. The roar rolls into ears and fills her head with confusion and pain, her brain pudding stirred by a maniac. A thunderstorm she tells herself. Rain will beat down on the wood-shingled or thatched or tiled roofs and the gray cobblestoned streets of Kolno, little silver geysers of water leaping from the pavement as joyfully as dancing Hasids, the stones gleaming under the spreading sheen of water that would lap at the statue of Lenin until it would dissolve like a pillar of salt. But the thunder is abnormally continuous, a steady syncopated drumbeat. Pressure balloons against the insides of her skull. She and Sarah Gittel run towards the market square and their house for shelter. Lenin still stands, frowning at the racket. Her house still stands, solidly waiting for them, its white walls flashing and crawling with light, but there are gaps like missing teeth in what was the row of houses along the border of the market square. Smoke pours out of windows like black sighs and flames dance in a malevolent glee.

A man floats down from the sky and lands in front of them, his boots striking the ground as if to root into it. For a second or a year he stands swaying, staring at them with brilliant green eyes flashing under the brim of his helmet, illuminated or blackened in the flashes of what she has come to realize are falling bombs. A black year, her mother screams. He grins, his teeth flashing as another bomb falls and brings his gun around but is yanked backwards by an Invisible Hand, dragged against the stones, lays still. Looking up, Raḥel sees white flowers opening their petals against the sky, other soldiers hanging and swaying beneath them. Dandelions. Red glowing streaks path from their dark forms to the ground and are answered by red streaks flashing up to the sky. A pilpul of fire. Dandelions bleed. All around her men are landing heavily, some on their feet, others falling over, their parachutes pulling them backwards or collapsing, covering the ground like tablecloths. Knives flash to cut the cords. She pulls her mother into the alley next to Maja's house, pounds on the door, then on the blue wooden window shutter painted with insanely cheerful white cyclamens. It remains shut. The walls around them shudder indignantly as more bombs fall. She and her mother lie down in the mud, holding each other. The night framed by the narrow walls of the alley is a black page scribbled with streaks of fire.

Chapter Twenty: Lenin's Funeral

Two weeks after the Germans came back, Raḥel returns one last time to the cemetery with a crowd of Jews bearing the statue of Lenin as if it were a corpse. Her mother's body on the other hand still lies in the shed of Andrej Gorecki, a steady customer who once upon a time had bought a wonderfully embroidered linen tablecloth from their market square stall for his daughter's wedding and who a week ago had wrapped his left hand around Sarah Gittel's forehead and pressed her to his chest while he sawed at her throat, that wonderful birthplace of imprecations and curses and wails against the injustices of the world and the stupidities of men, with the knife in his left hand. So Sarah Gittel, her mother who had given her to another woman's breasts to free herself, who had nourished and grown a secret crown of glory, who had stood and fearlessly demanded justice from authority, was defined finally as a half a kilo of sugar and a smile and a clap on the back given to Gorecki by one of the laughing Germans who watched.

The word "laughter," Raḥel thinks, like many other

words in the last two weeks had also changed its meaning. It was a revelation that words could contain their own antonyms. What was the good of words then? There were several other corpses in the shed—Raḥel has heard that some Poles had begun calling it the Yids' Tavern—but more corpses, Jews and some Russian soldiers, just left lying on the street or in the fields where golden stalks of grain scratched at their souls.

The word "Pole" has also changed its denotation, or at least devolved into differing connotations. In Kolno, there had been Polish farmers, drovers, musicians, thieves, aristocrats, predators, reformers, customers, suppliers, gamblers, whores, priests, nuns, poets and painters, tall Poles, short Poles, sick Poles, well Poles, beautiful Poles, Poles ugly as turnips, friendly Poles, unfriendly Poles, indifferent Poles, loving Poles. Now all the differentiations have been polished down to a terrible trinity: those Poles who would murder Jews or give them up to be murdered or those who would not and those who would hide them. No other differentiation exists anymore.

All words have been honed down to their simplest meaning, like many-faceted diamonds reduced to their origin coals.

Two weeks. *HaShem* had created the world and

mankind in seven days. The Germans destroyed it in two weeks. This time they had floated from the sky like dandelion seeds.

Since her mother's murder, she and Elazar had stayed hidden during the day in the cramped root cellar dug under the dirt floor of Wanda and Maja's house, the trap door entrance concealed by a rug they had brought from their house. Raḥel had thought of hiding in their own cellar, as the family had traditionally done during the more traditional spasms of mob murders. But the Germans had taken over the house on Zabriole Street soon after their arrival. She and Elazar huddled bent over a pile of potatoes, stewing in their own sweat, wrapped in their own stink and from the bucket used for their waste. During the night, they scavenged, stayed out of sight, tried to gauge what was happening.

Since her mother's murder. Since the end of Sarah Gittel. She cannot stop remembering the married woman's wig her mother had worn, how after the death of her husband, Sarah Gittel had let her hair grow under it, and then one day flung it off her head and into the fireplace. She and her mother had sat together and watched as the filaments of hair had glowed red as the wig writhed in the flame, as if it were a living thing. Raḥel had turned then to look at her mother's face, the slight smile on her lips, the reflection of the flames dancing in her eyes. Who is this woman, she had thought; the same question that burned in her mind when she saw her mother march braver than an army into the lairs of a cowardly priest and a courageous soldier. *Eshet chayil mee yimtza.* Who can find a woman of valor? How could all the complications of a person's life, the love, the turmoil, the bitterness she had covered herself with like the black shawl she wore on her head, as if all her life she had anticipated it would end so brutally, the strength, the yearned for secret self revealed when she threw away her wig; how could it be ended with such a terrible and abrupt punctuation?

How could the Germans be worse than the Russians? That rhetorical question she remembered being hotly debated in the market square has been resolved with appalling clarity. By the second day, more Germans had rolled into town on trucks and motorcycles. They pinned an edict on the door of the town hall ordering all Jews to wear the yellow star, forbidding them from going to public spaces or to be out anywhere after sunset. On the third day, they burned the synagogue, using the Torah scrolls as a torch and the sexton Yosef Abramov's bayoneted corpse as part of the kindling. By the time they burned *melamed* Chaim Szapiro's cheder and the Beit Midrash and the Kehilah, the office for the Jewish charity fund, everyone understood that the world had become a new planet. Kolno as Jew town was finished. There were three Jews to each Pole, as it had been for two hundred years, but now many of the Poles suddenly discovered that condition was intolerable. Anyway, a dead Jew was a bag of sugar and a smile of approval. Was a house, furniture, jewelry. As was a hidden Jew, discovered and turned in to the Germans. An arrogant Jew bitch who until now had never deigned to look at them was its own award, no bag of sugar needed.

On the day of Lenin's funeral, even in their hole, Raḥel and Elazar can hear harsh shouts, screams, fists pounding against doors, shots. The echoing voice of God announces through a bullhorn that all Jews must assemble in the market square.

If they find us, Elazar says, Wanda and Maja . . .

Raḥel nods. He needn't finish the sentence. Their Polish protectors would be killed.

But when they try to push up the trap door, it rises for an inch and then slams back down. They push again.

Be still, Maja says.

We can't stay here, Maja. They will kill you.

If you go they will kill you. You're safe here.

They'll search the house, Raḥel says. I've drunk from your breasts. Time to wean me into the world.

We will run to the forest, Elazar says. Join the Jewish partisans.

It had been Elazar's plan since he heard of the existence of such resistance groups. His own experience with the partisans had nearly cost his life. They would have murdered him as much for his circumsized *putz* as for his weapon.

But the group with whom he'd come in contact were anti-Semitic, fascist elements within the AK, the Home Guard, and he knew of other Jews who were fighting with the AK and the People's Army. Now there were all-Jewish bands as wall, with some of the fighters coming from the Bundist youth he had trained, others from HaShomer Hatzair, the Leftist Zionist Youth group in Lomza, which also for years had sent members to the forest for practice in farming and clandestine military training before immigrating to Palestine. They had been joined as well by the communists, and even right-wing Betar Zionists and religious Jews. As had happened to the Poles, the definition of who was a Jew had also been simplified and purified into linked dichotomies. Captured or hunted. Dead or alive. Fighter or victim.

Some of the Jews had been absorbed into Russian or Polish partisan units. Some were being murdered by other

Polish resistance groups. How would they know where to go, how to look, how to tell one from the other, Raḥel had asked. Her husband's silence was an answer.

Let them go, Wanda says, staring into Raḥel's eyes. Her Polish sister, nourished at the same breasts. She is weeping, pressing some clothing into Raḥel's arms. Two ragged jackets, a man's and a woman's, each with the Yellow Star sewed on it with ragged stitches, as if from a trembling hand. She embraces Raḥel, presses her lips to Raḥel's lips. If you're seen without these, she says.

They put on the jackets. Instead of the fear or vulnerability Raḥel had imagined she would feel when donning the Star, she feels embraced.

A stream of Jews is passing Maja's house, filling the narrow street. Raḥel can hear shouts, in German and in Polish, the crack of whips, screams. They open the door slightly, slip out of Christian Poland, rejoin their people. Some of whom are carrying sledge hammers, saws, and crow bars. They look, Raḥel thinks, like a revolutionary poster. Workers of the world unite. Anger and hope boils in her chest. But on second look, the way people are carrying the tools is desultory, not as if they are weapons. Not even as if they were tools. Was this another labor *antel*? Against which new enemy would they again be digging trenches?

As they begin to enter the cleared market square, checker-boarded with the rectangle impressions of burnt stalls, she turns to the girl next to her, Esther Abramsky, a seamstress, sixteen years old, to ask. Esther turns to her and starts to speak. The crack of a whip explodes next to her ear; the whip itself lashes across the girl's mouth, her lips exploding. She clutches her face, her fingers outlined in blood; the whip lashes her shoulders. Elazar shouts, starts forward, but she clutches his arm, his muscles twitching like a mad stallion's in her grip. Pulling him back. Poles, her neighbors, are whipping or beating people with clubs. A line of German soldiers stands behind them, their weapons pointed at the Jews, who shuffle forward heads bent, like people leaning into a strong wind. Motorcycles mounted with machine guns anchor both ends of their line, one barrel pointed directly at her. She searches the Germans' faces, looking for what? Compassion? Disturbance? A mirrored humanity? Two Poles have grabbed Jakub Bernsztajn, a tailor, by the arms. Another Pole, she recognizes the drayman Fyodor Ziembinski, who'd always had sweets in his pocket for her and her brother, grips Jakub's hair, pulls his head back and cuts his throat. A collective moan goes up from the Jews.

It comes to Raḥel that all of them, Poles and

Germans, must be possessed by dybbuks. More of her fellow townsmen hover behind the German soldiers. They have brought sausages, bottles of beer and vodka, their children. Laughing. Pointing, as if at favorite players in a game. Basil Sokolinski, another customer she recognizes, grabs Esther; she is still pressing her palms, fingers outlined in blood, to her face. A knife flashes, but all he cuts is her clothing; in a moment she is naked, moving her hands down to cover herself. He starts to pull her away. Elazar shakes off Raḥel's grip and steps forward, grabs Esther's arm, pulls her back. Sokolinski curses at him, steps forward, the knife raised over his head. Raḥel can envision what will occur, Elazar striking Sokolinski's face with his boxer's fist, her husband cut down in a flurry of stabbing.

The voice of God booms out again, freezing the scene. Whatever is said swells and echoes, the words distorted. But it is only, she sees, a lanky German soldier speaking harshly into a megaphone. Perhaps that, finally, truly is the true Voice of *HaShem,* she thinks. At least it has stopped her husband, though not Sokolinski, who now yanks the sobbing girl away from the crowd, pulls her towards the row of houses. She grabs hold of Elazar, who has surged forward again. She is not alone. Other hands reach out, grab him, hold him back. They killed her parents the first day,

Elazar says, his face red with the effort to break free, And will murder you and your pregnant wife and how many more of us if you try to fight them, says Beryl Epsteyn, his arm draped around Elazar's neck. As if to punctuate his words, a German soldier fires three shots from his rifle into the air.

Dybbuks.

It is the only explanation for them, these countrymen of Bach, Beethoven, and Goethe.

Lenin is your God, the dybbuk with the megaphone shouts into it, in Polish. Lenin is your God and your God is dead.

She is confused for a second and then sees the dybbuk is standing in front of the treasure left to Kolno by the Russians and blamed now, she understands, on the Jews. The statue of Vladimir Illych Lenin. His blind eyes staring into the future.

Your God Lenin is dead, the Voice of God booms. The time has come to bury him, right in the Yid boneyard, where he belongs. The dybbuk points the cone-shaped megaphone at the statute; the other dybbuks point their weapons at the Jews, who for a few seconds stare at them, uncertain what to do. A Hasid, Mendel Gurrah, steps towards the line of soldiers, a question on his face, his right hand in the air, forefinger extended, as if he were going to argue a Talmudic point. The dybbuk with the megaphone shifts the instrument to his left hand, draws out a pistol with his right, and shoots Mendel Gurrah in the head. A part of Mendel stings Raḥel's cheek. People are screaming, weeping, but stand frozen in fear. There are silver skulls on the dybbuk's black collar and in the front of the peaked hat he wears. He has a narrow, severe, very young-looking face and the skulls make him look to her like a boy playing pirate. Skull, she thinks. The dybbuk is named Skull. Her father had always laughed at her habit of giving everyone nicknames. The Fox. The Red Hen. The Long Drink of Water. The Loose *Kreplach.* What hit her face must have been a part of Mendel Gurrah's skull. Skull raises the pistol again. Work you fucking parasites, he screams.

Elazar yanks a sledge hammer from the grip of Herman Wolkowicz, who stands swaying helplessly, looking dazed. Her husband swings the hammer against Lenin's legs. Almost immediately others join him, swarming the statue, striking it with hammers, trowels, even rocks, taking their impotent rage out on the unfeeling stone of the statue. Some, tool-less, claw at it bare-handed. The Polish onlookers are laughing and cursing, their faces flushed red. More black clad, helmeted dybbuks arrive; their whips crack in the air, strike against bent backs or legs or upturned faces.

The dybbuks already there remain standing grim-faced, their rifles still pointed. Mendel Gurrah's head bleeds out into the street; Raḥel, unable to stop staring, sees it collapsing inwards, like a deflating balloon. She can't tell if she is really seeing it. For an instant it transforms into the child in her womb, ripped out of her, melting into blood on the cobblestones. As if sharing her vision, the baby kicks frantically against its confining space. She tears her eyes away, goes to the statue, starts tearing at it with her hands, the stone cold against her palms, its broken edges cutting into her flesh. Lenin looks down at her sternly, reproachfully.

Skull holds his megaphone up and pushes it in the direction of the watching, jeering Poles. Bring carts, fools, he screams in Polish. Bring carts, bring hearses, bring a fucking palanquin—don't you understand that this is a fucking funeral?

Some of the Poles run off towards the livery stables where the horses her family owned or boarded still stand, placidly and indifferent to human affairs. Two wooden carts are pulled and pushed up to the base of the statues; the Jews start throwing parts of Lenin into them as Skull sings into the megaphone:

Because of the Jew

The war came to you

But golden Hitler arrived

And made him work . . .

The Poles join in a ragged chorus, grinning or laughing out loud, something in them liberated. Raḥel stares at their faces, these men and women she had known all her life. Possessed by dybbuks as well. It must be. But not all of them. Behind their line, in the window of a two-story house, she sees a Polish friend, Halina Golshovska, her face framed by a helmet of blond braids. Their eyes meet. Halina is weeping, mouthing something to Raḥel. Sorrow? Apologies? Shame? Halina's husband Piotr, appears in the window frame, his face grim; he pulls Halina away.

Lenin's head, now detached, lies face up on the peak of the pile of rubble in one cart, eyes clouded with yellow dust.

What are you waiting for, mother-fucking Yids? Onwards! To the cemetery! Skull screams into his megaphone, his voice echoing in feedback. We will bury the red motherfucker and then we'll bury you! Elazar and three other men take up positions along the wagon tongue; they pull, straining against the weight; others get behind the cart and push, heading the procession. They move out of the market square and down Vincenty Street, past the looted, desecrated synagogue. The whips crack the air. Chaim Glazer, a tanner, raises his right arm as the tip of a whip snaps near his eyes; he grips it as it wraps around his wrist and then grabs the rawhide with his other hand and yanks it from the dybbuk's hand. In the same instance, the other dybbuks open fire, exploding Chaim's chest, and striking down two people, a man and a woman, on either side of him. Everyone else freezes. The three corpses lie on the stones; Chaim's right hand, still upraised as when he blocked the whip, echoes the forearm and hand of Lenin, detached and upright in the rubble in the cart. A helmeted dybbuk pries the whip from the dead man's grasp, looks around, hands it to one of Raḥel's cousins, Yankel Brikman. Whip, you son of a bitch, he screams in Yankel's face, her cousin, a cheder boy, stands still, the whip dangling helplessly from his hand, imitating the sidelocks dangling around his face. The dybbuk, transforming back and forth in Raḥel's eyes into a soldier with long flaxen hair and a long pale face marked with red pimples, into a dybbuk, into a soldier, into a boy, snatches the whip and begins beating Yankel around the shoulders, the boy still not moving, shuddering in pain. The dybbuk pushes the whip handle back into the boy's hand.

Yankel begins laying it around him, his eyes shut. A snap slashes open a wound on a woman's face. Some of the other dybbuks, laughing, handed whips to other Jews and then stood back, pointing their rifles at the crowd, as the Jews whip their fellows.

At the end of the street, they turn left onto Senkevitz Street, towards the cemetery, the Polish mob surging along with them, on either side, jeering, laughing, hurling stones and pieces of rubble. Other Poles, in the houses along the street, stare from the windows, though some turn their faces away in shame and others draw their shutters closed or their curtains together, their faces stricken. A young woman Raḥel does not know, equally pregnant, stares at her, her face streaked with tears. A red-bearded man Raḥel recognizes as a postman who would bring mail to their house, frowns at the woman and then slaps her face, left-side, right-side and then crosses himself. They are passing the cheder and the horse market, as if passing by the landmarks of their lives. Dybbuks lash the Jews, man, woman, or child. She sees Chaim Szapiro join the procession from the cheder and she understands fully now the lessons Szapiro passed on to her even though she was a girl, the lessons that the crack of those whips are writing in the air and onto that brethren flesh. She touches the yellow star

Maja had sewn on her coat. It does not matter who you are or what you do. What you are is the target of whips. It does not matter if you are a child or a man or a woman or rich or poor or a horse trader or a shopkeeper or a sharpener of knives or a tanner of hides or a merciful forgiver of debts or a merciless collector or a child who dreams of flying or a Torah scholar or a yeshiva bochur or an atheist or a communist or a Zionist or a hater of all politics. It does not matter that you are loved or hated or if you are lovers or coveters of your neighbors' wives or husbands. It does not matter that you were named after a beloved grandfather or grandmother or a holy prophet of God. It does not matter that once you allowed your woman's fierce mane to grow until you could tear the wig off your head and demand of an enemy that he acts like a human being. It does not matter that you have a name because you don't have a name or perhaps it is only and always the same name. Your name is Whip Me. Your life has become circular and simple. You are a thing to be whipped. Or throat-cut. Or raped. Or shot down in the street, as she sees happen now to Avrum and Hoda Feinsheim as they try to run away as the procession turns into the street leading to the cemetery. A Pole, a dybbuk she doesn't know snatches their baby, a boy, as Hoda falls, and holding it by its ankles, swings it, dashing its head against the cobblestones, tossing it aside like garbage. Is this too much? Is this impossible? Over the crack of the whips she hears the answer in a volley of gunshots, hears a moan burst from the mouths of the marchers, the bearers of stones to the graveyard, feels a shudder run through their flesh into her flesh and into the body of her unborn child.

Ahead of her, she sees her husband, struggling against the weight of rubble in the wagon. She thinks of her friend Halina's face as if in a distant memory of childhood in another country. A golden country. She thinks of the expression on Lenin's stone, dust-caked, broken face. Apologies? Sorrow? Shame?

At the cemetery, the soldiers make them pull the cart in over gravestones, sledge-hammering those in the way of its path. The cart bumps up as if over piles of bones, hundreds of years of dead Jews in this place, Jews who had brought with them all they had learned about staying alive as they fled other massacres and blood libels and humiliations to this point on earth.

Seeing the cart bumping over her ancestors' bones Raḥel comes to understand how their wisdom, all the learning she had eaten like a feast at her father's table and at the table of the *melamed* Chaim Szapiro, the history she had wanted to sink into so she could know her place in the world where she was forced to sojourn, the wisdom of wandering and enduring she had thought to draw into herself, has been rendered useless. For those around her in this mad exodus. For herself. In her life, she had hidden with her family as mobs surged through the town, burning Jewish houses and shops, killing and raping, even at the moment her own body had begun to bleed, as if it had been awakened to the fact of her womanhood by the blood flowing in the gutters before her house. She had seen the same mob then, hooting, screaming hatred, the spittle flying from their mouths, as she sees in the streets of her town today. They had been a storm that passed, as was the nature of storms. Some of her people fought it anyway, but most hid, or keep their faces blank, as not to meet eyes, stayed out of the way, cringed, laughed uneasily at the jokes, ignored the talk of the blood of Christian children baked into matzos, the accusations of limitless wealth and power, of revolutionary subversion, the Accusation of Deicide, for which they were crucified for the crucifixion of one of their own. The storm would pass. They followed the wisdom inscribed in their flesh and minds and souls by decades and millennia of slaughter and expulsion, a dark procession whose shape was revealed when lit by the flaming bodies bound to the stakes of the Spanish

Inquisition, by the raped and mutilated of Chelmieki the Cossack's massacres, the Black Hundreds, the Russian pogroms. The same mob, timeless, screams at them now, whips them now, kills them now even as they desecrate the graves of their dead, and these Jews, her brothers and sisters, think they know with the wisdom of thousands of years that still many of them would live, and those that lived would go back into their lives and build them again and have children and find again the passions and distractions of the living in family and children or God or in Man or in Profit or Ideology or the enjoyment of a meal. They would search for a meaning in their existence. Or not. They would, in a word, live. The storm would pass.

But Raḥel knows now that they are lying to themselves. That is the wisdom revealed to her, as if she were the prophetess, Miriam. They would not live. Not this time. This is the end of their history in this place. This was the wisdom the bones were confiding in her, in her own bones, whispering into the tiny beautifully-formed ear of the fetus floating in her womb, as if her womb is a Genizah, as if the child floats in a repository of all the stories of their ancestors, the stories it should have carried into the world and then forgotten, the child whispering into the whisper of her blood.

Skull orders them to stop. The other dybbuks train their weapons on the Jews like a promise.

Skull scans the crowd, looking for something, and then shoves a man aside, goes to grab a shovel from Yaakov Rabinovich. For a second, Yaakov hangs on; in that instance before he releases the tool the German points his pistol at his face. Yaakov steps back, hands raised. Skull grins, taps him lightly on the forehead with the gun barrel, screams at the crowd to give shovels to the men he calls pall-bearers. When he hands Elazar the shovel he took from Yaakov, Raḥel sees her husband's knuckles whitening as he grips the handle, the tension in his shoulders and she is certain he will swing the shovel into the German's face. She steps forward, a small cry escaping her lips, catching Elazar's eye, shaking her head. He stands for the barest instance, torn by the tension she can see in the tremble in his arm, the knowledge of his power, his boxer's tension between needing to smash into the man's teeth and the frantic no in his wife's eyes, the presence of the child in her womb, the need to cling even if only moments longer to the quick of life. She knows this. She knows these dybbuks will not let them live; they will all be as buried as the statue of Lenin, now being tossed into the hole her husband and the other pall bearers have dug. She knows in her bones that to go along, to obey in order to live is an illusion, that the air she feels going into her nostrils, rich with the smell of turned earth, sharp with the odors of sweat-fear from the people around her, from herself, is only borrowed. But she can't bring herself to let it go, not even if this is the last instance of it, to see Elazar taken from her, no matter how much she wants to see the edge of that shovel re-shaping the skull grin on the Skull's face.

Rabbi, step forward, Skull says. Then screams it. Chaim Szapiro steps forward, accepting the burden of the title. Rabbi Dayan, she knows from his absence, must be dead or in hiding. Skull seizes Szapiro's beard, yanks him to the edge of the hole.

Nu, Skull says, in an exaggerated Yiddish accent. *Doven. Doven*, Rabbi. The prayer for the dead.

He waves his pistol at the crowd of Jews. Mourn, you cunts. The way you do it. Let me see you rocking, the way you do, Yids. Let me hear you sing. Let me see you sway like you're on a fucking boat. He brings the megaphone to his lips with one hand and sings his song again:

Because of the Jew
The war came to you

As he sings, he brings the pistol to Szapiro's forehead, pushes the barrel against it.

But golden Hitler arrived
And made him die . . . .

At the last word, Szapiro begins the mourner's Kaddish. Behind him, some of the others murmur the Aramaic words or chant them. She knows the words, even knows their meaning. *Yitgadal v'yitkadash sh'mei raba b'alma di-v'ra chirutei, v'yamlich malchutei b'chayeichon uvyomeichon uvchayei d'chol beit yisrael, ba'agala uvizman kariv, v'im'ru: amen*, the *melamed* sings, his voice barely above a whisper, the "amen" from the crowd only a whisper also, bracketed by groans. *Glorified and sanctified be God's great name throughout the world which He has created according to His will. May He establish His kingdom in your lifetime and during your days, and within the life of the entire House of Israel, speedily and soon; and say, Amen.*

Swallowed and be-shat be Skull throughout the world which He has created according to His will, Raḥel thinks. Amen.

Sing, you cocksuckers! Skull screams. Szapiro looks

at him, meets his eyes. As the German raises his pistol, Szapiro raises his voice: *Y'hei sh'mei raba m'varach l'alam ul'almei almaya.Yitbarach v'yishtabach, v'yitpa'ar v'yitromam v'yitnaseh, v'yithadar v'yit'aleh v'yit'halal sh'mei d'kud'sha, b'rich hu, l'eila min-kol-birchata v'shirata, tushb'chata v'nechemata da'amiran b'alma, v'im'ru: amen. May His great name be blessed forever and to all eternity. Blessed and praised, glorified and exalted, extolled and honored, adored and lauded be the name of the Holy One, blessed be He, beyond all the blessings and hymns, praises and consolations that are ever spoken in the world; and say, Amen.*

Glorified and exalted, extolled, and honored, adored and lauded? Raḥel spits. For this? For *ha-yom ha-zeh?* For this day he brings us to? For these days. These people are insane. Her people. She has seen the Face of *Elohim.* It is the Face of a Skull.

Szapiro has closed his eyes and is singing loudly and clearly and the people have raised their voices also, and their shoulders are swaying and tears run down faces; they are mourning themselves.

May his name turn to shit and dirt and may he grow like an onion with his head in the earth forever and to all eternity, Raḥel thinks. May he go shit in the ocean, amen.

Szapiro's voice rises, strongly, fervently, the Jews around him, around Raḥel, even her Elazar, repeating the words, clinging to the words, the need to rise with the words swelling their chests: *May there be abundant peace from heaven, and life, for us and for all Israel; and say, Amen. He who creates peace in His celestial heights, may He create peace for us and for all Israel; and say, Amen.*

May He who plays with our lives as does Skull, may He who brings us to this place and to these days taste the bitterness of ashes in His Mouth. May His right hand wither. May His Cock fall off. Amen.

A part of her is aware and afraid of what she is doing. She is cursing God. But then again, she thinks, what could He do to her? Send her to be born in Kolno? She touches her belly. Send her a child to be born in Kolno?

But the people are singing loudly all around her, the ancient words liberating something in their breasts; their eyes closed, their shoulders swaying in desert rhythms. She sees that the Poles clustered around the edge of the cemetery have grown silent; they shuffle uneasily. The dybbuks have raised their rifles, but the whips hang loosely in the hands of those with whips.

Enough, Skull screams. Enough! He raises his pistol in the air and shoots. The Jews continue to sing and now

Raḥel joins them, joins with their words, the ancient words, not the words that had felt bitter as acid on her tongue, burning into it before they could be released into the world.

Enough, the Skull screams.

He raises his pistol and shoots Szapiro in the mouth. The *melamed's* last words transmute into the stream of blood that gushes out. This is prayer, thinks Raḥel. This is prayer in its physical form. This is prayer and its answer. This is our dialogue with *HaShem.* Jews scream in anguish or in anger, some weep, some moan, but collectively they step forward, tools raised, towards the Skull. For an instant Raḥel sees a moth of fear flutter in his eyes, but he raises the pistol and shoots again, into the crowd, and there are more shots from the other dybbuks, and again the crack of the whips. The people who still stand freeze and stand as still as the corpses on the ground. He points the pistol at Elazar.

Run, you motherfuckers. It is past curfew, why are you here? Run!

Elazar grasps her hand. As he once had from the back of a horse. They run. The Jews disperse in all directions, as if the cemetery is vomiting out its dead, leaving inert shapes lying patiently in the cemetery dirt, as if waiting their turn for burial. She grabs her husband's arm, yanks it, and he turns and they are running through the streets of their town, along the obscene normality of the road where they had carted goods, or rode in fancy buggies, or sat for the first time in an automobile, or sauntered, dressed in their best through the lace of leaf shadows from the poplars lining the street they seemed able to feel brushing their skin like a blessing, to visit friends or family; through the alleys where they had played as children, past closed doors and windows behind which they had eaten and drank and talked and laughed. As the sun sank, those who didn't die, ran. Under the staccato of gunfire, the crack of whips, the enthusiastic cheers of the Poles, an audience of critics freed to murder the players they'd hated or envied for so long.

Chapter Twenty-One: Bread

The night is soft, quilted cotton. Raḥel feels its folds brush her face. It wraps her as she had once been wrapped in the linen her father smuggled over the border. The feeling as fragile as mist, as childish wishes, as children's tales in *Grininke Beymelekh* that ended in happy-ever-after. She is vulnerable, exposed, the child inside her pushing and kicking against the wall of her abdomen as if in rebellion against her sudden desire to surrender, rest, lie down and die. She and Elazar are shadows within shadows, separated from the town where they had been born and lived as if they already were in the other world.

They duck into an alley off Gromatzin Street. The rear door of a house at its far end is open, banging against the wall at its side. A rhomboid of light from inside forms and disappears on the cobblestones as the door repeatedly opens and closes. Fear hums in a current through her stomach. It is past curfew and the door should be closed, locked. She and Elazar melt into the alley wall, next to two stacked pickle barrels. She knows the house; it belongs to

Lev Dulovich, a widower, a talented baker with twin daughters, Amirah and Chava Dulovich, both fifteen. When she told them she was pregnant, a hundred years before, they had laid their hands flat on her stomach at the same time, as if they were one person, and she had thought how wonderful it must be to sense the world twice, to be doubled. Their faces had assumed an identical solemnity that made it seem as if their age had doubled as well and a thirty-year-old woman was touching and blessing her child.

The door swings open again. A thick, amorphous blackness moves out from the door and resolves into the Lewandowski brothers, drovers and drunkards. They stagger into the alley, laughing at their own stumbling, Alekssy clapping his brother Bozdar on the back and then suddenly doubling over, puking against the wall. Had they come for the bread or for the baker? This is where she would usually see the brothers, in front of her in line when she would be sent to the bakery for Lev's delicious black bread or, on the Sabbath, for his *challah,* so sweet the memory of it, even at this instant, causes her to salivate. Like many of his customers, the brothers bought on credit; she had heard the girls complain they never paid what they owed; their father was too kind, too forgiving of debts, too soft-hearted to cut them off. Sometimes we sell bread, their father would say, sometimes bread sells us. Think of it as rent. They didn't understand what he meant, they told Raḥel.

Still laughing, the two brothers stand unsteadily and piss against the wall. She and Elazar stay flattened against the opposite wall, next to the protecting shoulder of the barrels. Their piss smells acrid; its odor stings her nostrils. The brothers stagger away, their laughter swelling up and filling the narrow alley and then growing dimmer. Raḥel moves towards the open door, but Elazar grabs her arm, pulls her behind him and gets to the door first. He arrests its swing, looks inside. She pushes past him, her feet slipping on something wet, and then the thick, fecund smell of the blood plugging her nostrils. Lev Dulovich is tied to a chair, his face looking to the ceiling, the slash on his throat a terrible smile. A piece of paper is pinned to his chest by a knife, perhaps the same one that cut his throat. It looks to be a page from a ledger, a column of numbers listed on it. Amounts owed. Across from him the two girls, Amirah and Chava, are on the floor, naked and spreadeagled, pools of blood at their crotches and puddled under their heads and necks; their throats had also been cut. One of them—she can't tell who—had something white bulging out of her vagina; when Raḥel looks closer she recognized the rounded end of a loaf. Too hard for *challah*, she thinks, the absurd words coming into her mind in time for her to keep them from spilling from her lips, though not the wave of bile that followed, her vomit mixing with the blood on the floor. They had tied Lev so he had to watch. He could have closed his eyes, she thinks. But then she looks back at his eyes and sees why he couldn't.

We must go, Elazar says.

Where, she asks. She means where could they possibly go and not see the baker and his daughters, Szapiro's last gush of prayer, the baby dashed against the cobblestones, their unburied neighbors lying like stones on her father's grave, the faces of their other neighbors twisted into masks of hate or masks of pity as if those marked the poles, not tragedy or comedy, that encompassed human choices?

To the forest, is all her husband says.

Chapter Twenty-Two: Strength

After her father returned from the forest, after his stroke, before the true history of her life had begun; before Elazar and Argamaka and boxcars and Nazis and Lenin and dybbuks, it had been for her as if she'd become a small girl again, lying at her father's side and twining the wiry curls of his beard while he caressed her hair, and sometimes it is was if her father had become her child, lying helpless, his eyes wide and amazed, his other arm stiff at his side. The house was so cold their breaths were visible, twisting in the air. Above their heads were the potatoes, the only charity Sarah Gittel allowed the family to take. Raḥel tried to imagine she and her father are under the earth, the roots of plants growing over and around them, closing them in a living center of warmth, or that they are still hiding underground holding each other as they had when two armies clashed over their heads.

Hunger pinched her insides and throat. After her father had come back from the forest, helped by the good Polish farmer Mikhail Tcharnetzki, a small delegation of women from the Jewish Women's Aid Society had come to the house. Sarah Gittel opened the door and stood on top of the concrete stoop, cold and thin-faced in her black silk dress. She'd stared, her mouth a tight closed line, as they'd talked softly to her until Raḥel, watching from a window, could see her silence spread over them, one after another. Finally, they looked at each other, turned and walked away. Sarah Gittel closed the door without a word. The next morning, a basket of potatoes had been left anonymously on the stoop. Another had appeared each Shabbat. Who knows where potatoes come from, Sarah Gittel said, taking them inside.

Eating potatoes, selling them in the market square were all that kept them alive. Her brother, Yitzhak, was feverish, his wound refusing to heal; her father's right arm was frozen at his side, his voice frozen in his throat. He grunted and emitted desperate trapped sounds that broke her heart and make her mother turn away with a kind of satisfied disgust.

Every morning, Raḥel piled the sled with charity potatoes and sold or traded what she could, standing amid the burned and smashed stalls.

But who could buy anything? In the afternoon, Wanda, the daughter of the wet nurse Maja who had suckled

Raḥel the first five years of her life, came to look at the potatoes. She picked one up, then another, weighing each in the palm of her hand, examining each closely.

They're potatoes, Wanda.

You'd better be careful, Wanda said. Dogs bark. Who are jealous. Who growl about a house full of treasure that they somehow missed during the pogrom. Whisper about a dead man in the forest, on the smugglers' route, hidden gold.

Raḥel pointed to the blackened potatoes.

Here's our gold, Wanda, all we have.

Peasants grow potatoes, Jews grow money, Wanda shrugged.

Raḥel thought of the money her brothers Herman and Max had sent from America, growing under the floorboards, and flushed.

Your mother, for example, Wanda said, a woman who could pay someone else to be her breasts.

It made me your sister.

A sister who took milk from my mouth.

Raḥel stared at her. Wanda stares back, tossing her blond braids defiantly. Another changeling of this winter, a new flag.

When she told of her conversation with Wanda,

Sarah Gittel stared at her with burning eyes, a mocking expression of amazement on her face, as if to say: and this surprises you?

Why did you give me to Wanda's mother?

So you wouldn't suck me dry.

Mama, we have money.

American money. Dream money.

We can spend it.

Only for what its intended. She patted the handkerchief she kept always pinned inside her blouse. In it were the two toes her son Dov had chopped off his own foot. Sarah Gittel was going to bring them with her if they went to America.

We can't eat what's left of Dov.

Sarah Gittel brought her face close. Her breath stank coldly of potatoes.

Then be a stone. Stones don't need to eat.

She gestured upstairs, at her husband's room.

We have enough to leave. But can we put that weight on a sled and drag it after us?

Be quiet. He may hear. He protected you like a queen all your life.

Queens don't sit in the dark, eating rotten potatoes. Are you his wife now, to protect him?

That night when Raḥel lay in her bed, next to her groaning brother, she yearned to assume the delirium of Yitzhak's fever. It was a way to fly. Fly to America, a place where all shapes were possible. Dov was on his way, perhaps he was there already. He had put his bare foot on the stump outside and chopped off two of his toes to avoid being taken by the army; when they were going to arrest him anyway, he'd flown, light and unanchored. She understood his need to escape, the swift chop of the ax, the quick, necessary severance from the trap. Yet her father had been felled by a stroke, as if struck by the arc of the same ax. As if it were swinging back and forth, swiping away the men in her family: Yitzhak injuring his hand and his flesh starting to rot, festering from the dirt and damp of the earthen cellar in which they'd hid during the pogrom. Her father had dragged him in the sled to a doctor, pulling him mid-winter and mid-war through thick crusts of snow in a forest of black frozen branches, full of wolves, bandits, and deserters. He'd brought Yitzhak back with his son's hand cleaned and stitched, saved, but with his own coat stiff with blood and his own right arm frozen and dead, as if given in trade. Rahel thought for the first time in years of her sister Bechele, carried away by the flu. She had been struck first, before Bechele, burning with the fever that had taken away half the children of Kolno. She'd felt her soul already slipping out, light as a silken thread, unraveling her into mist. But her sister had come to her in that mist and smiled and touched her forehead, and she felt the thick hot worm of the sickness loosen from her heart. That night Bechele had taken to her bed and never rose. The smile was still on her face, left behind, better than toes, a clipped wing.

Papa, what should I do, where should I go?

You're not a stone. Fly.

I'm not a bird either.

You're my daughter, a smuggler's daughter. There are secret paths through the forest, I'll tell you about them. May He who blessed Sarah, Rebekah, Leah and Rachel, Miriam the prophetess and Esther the Queen, Master of the World, may he bless you. Hazak hazak v'nit'hazek. *Strength and more strength.*

The voice was so strong in her head she had to go to her father's room. He lay staring at his dead arm as if it were alien flesh grafted to his shoulder. He turned his stare to her. *Papa, where should I go?* His pale face glowed in a patch of moonlight, eyes dark holes above a dark beard. The lips frozen into a rictus smile. The arm, twitching like a wing, began to rise. Higher and then higher. Raḥel watched as he gathered himself and pulled his arm out of the sleeve of death. The moonlight bathed it. The fingers curled into a claw, slowly straightened. Pointed out of the window, to the moon.

Chapter Twenty-Three: The Piska Forest

She feels that arm rising now, as if from her heart, follows that finger pointing to life into her father's forest. She hears the whisper of the Lavnes and a second later they see it, a twisted silver ribbon against the black backdrop of the night. It begins to rain, the drops pattering the river at first, and then as the downpour starts, awakening an undulating forest of silver geysers. The baby moves again inside her as they go into the water, sinking to their waists, the mud clutching their feet, trying to suck her shoes off.

The trees encompass them. But do not confuse her. She had often accompanied her father on his smuggling trips; she knew the skein of secret trails through forest that seemed thick and solid as a wall when the eyes fell on it. As solid and impenetrable as the row of houses along Zabielo Street, their street along the market square would seem, if one didn't know all the people in each house, their faces, their laughter and tears, their secrets: the Abramowitzs, the Dulovichs, the Moussieffs, the Lobels, the Lobels, the

Lobels, the Brikmans, the Brikmans, the Brikmans. Pines, live oaks, locust trees, elms, birch. Ivy, crawlers, skunk cabbage, blueberry bushes, where to find the patches of mushrooms shaded by ferns; how to tell which were poisonous, which could be eaten. Thank you, Papa.

At night, now, the thickness could be felt, the forest only seen in glimpses of tree trunks silvered by moonlight where brief openings in the leaf canopy let the light leak in. She leads now; Elazar does not object. She prays. Lets the pressing growth she feels in the living things around her root into her womb; lets the forest surround the memories of this day, of these days, press them down, obscure them, hide them, strangle them. It is sometime in July; she no longer knows the date, but she can feel the riotous fecundity, the heat pressing like fingers on their skin, sweat feeling like a band pressed around her forehead. She feels her child kick inside her, lays a hand on her abdomen. The sweat has soaked through her clothes; it wets her palm. Has it mixed with the amniotic fluid cushioning her child, weeping out through her flesh?

She remembers the winter her brother Yitzhak had injured his hand badly with an axe and became feverish and her father had pulled him on a sled through this forest to a doctor he knew over the border. A German, during a time when that name meant educated, refined, civilized, the antonym of Cossack or Muzhak. On the way back, he had been stopped, threatened by an army deserter who had been hiding in the forest, robbing and often murdering travelers. Raḥel knew that much, but the details of how her father, and Yitzhak, had escaped the man were never spoken of in the family. How do you think we got away, Yitzhak had said to her years later. What choice do you think Papa had? Her brother had been feverish, and what he witnessed had the quality of a fragmented fever dream, Papa transformed to a shining, terrible angel, the arc of an axe swing through the air a fiery silver path punctuated by the solid thunk of the blow. Later, when Papa had his stroke, he lost his ability to speak and walk, and his right arm lay paralyzed, dead as a stick at his side. It was only when Yitzhak confirmed to her what had happened that the thought came to her that it was the arm that had wielded the axe. One day, when she was sitting next to him, he slowly, sweat springing to his forehead, pulled his arm out of the sleeve of paralysis and pointed out of the window at the moon. She had known what he was telling her then, and she knows it now, looking at the moon through a gap in the tree canopy

You're my daughter, a smuggler's daughter. There are secret paths through the forest, I'll tell you about them.

In the dark between the trees, her mind wanders down such lanes into the past, as if searching different escape routes than those her body follows now. Memory seems the more realistic destination. Where could they go?

Tcharnetzki, her husband says. She realizes she had asked the question out loud. She stops, looks at Elazar. He shrugs.

You've mentioned him. His place can't be far from here. We can't stumble through the dark, hunting for partisans. If we can have a night . . .

She touches her abdomen. Strength and more strength.

Mikhail Tcharnetzki, a farmer, had often visited the Brikmans whenever he came to trade his produce at the market square; he was one of the few Poles they invited to join Shabbat dinners. A widower with no children, he'd become friendly after buying a pair of plough horses that her brother Dov had brought over the border from East Prussia. When her father, his arm paralyzed from murder, was returning with Yitzhak from the German doctor, Tcharnetzki had helped them to get home.

Once he had even celebrated Purim with them, bringing *groggers,* noise-makers he'd fashioned from dried gourds filled with pebbles; they delighted the children and had at last even couched a smile from Sarah Gittel's tight mouth. He'd known enough to paint the forms of the cousin-heroes, Esther and Mordecai, the Persian King Ahasuerus sporting a long, black flag of a beard that resembled the farmer's own, and a villainous Haman with sly, foxlike features on the gourds. The farmer seemed to regard his visits as if they were journeys to an exotic foreign land, smiling and nodding constantly, touching everyday objects in the house and muttering as if they were holy relics. He spoke with them in a mixture of Yiddish and Polish that Raḥel had dubbed "horse;" the ins and outs, customs, personalities and vagaries, delights and diseases of that species being the main concern of his conversations with her father and brother. She remembers now that he had named the twin plough horses Esther and Mordecai.

She touches Elazar's face. Follow this path, she says. Maybe he will give us a *se'udat Purim,* a Purim feast.

I'd settle for a glass of vodka. With or without the glass. Come, be careful. He lifts a branch full of thorns over her head.

Bessarabian wine, she thinks. That's what they had drunk, at that Purim feast. Bessarabian wine smuggled from Odessa, downed during that holiday when one was encouraged to get drunk, the men anyway. Though that night she had been given enough of a taste to get giddy. That holiday when one was enjoined to be merry and celebrate, once again, the miraculous survival of the Jews, the destruction of their enemies.

The path opens into the farm yard. The thatched roof house, the small outhouse, the barn stark black and white representations of themselves in the silver moonlight. An illustration in a book. Should they wake Tcharnetzki or just sneak into his barn without disturbing him? Elazar whispers.

Disturb him, Raḥel says. She is still imaging the taste of that Purim meal, of biting into the warm, crisp dough of the *hamentashen*, tri-cornered like Haman's hat, her mouth flooded with the warmth of the poppy-seed filling. Haman, who was hung for plotting to murder the Jews. Would Skull have the same fate, his death celebrated by Jews drunk with Bessarabian wine and rescued life, their children costumed with yellow stars, shaking rattles made of gourds and pebbles? She does not believe it. The thought comes to her that the child in her belly will never feel his mouth fill with the taste of warm dough and poppy seeds.

It wrenches a moan from her throat. She has held it all inside her, clenched around the memories of that day as if squeezing them in a fist, until she and her husband stepped into this farmyard. Into this picture mono-colored into an instant memory of itself, seen the way a ghost might remember life.

Elazar turns to her, but he asks no question when he sees her face, her shaking shoulders, only wraps his arms around her, drawing her to him. She stays, enveloped in his warmth for a moment, an hour, a year, and then pushes him slightly away, reaches up to his chest and rips off the yellow star. He nods, tears the star off her coat.

A light shines into her eyes, blinding her. She feels a lurch of panic in her chest, for an instant is filled with the senseless conviction that the act of pulling off their stars had instantly brought the Germans to them, as if it has sent a vibration in the air tuned to their senses. As if they were all-powerful. She hears her name, spoken like a question.

Raḥel?

It is Tcharnetzki, holding up a lantern. He is standing bandy-legged, wearing only a long night shirt and boots, his broad, kind face, framed by a crown of wildly uncombed hair and a black beard, looking at her with an expression of concern that makes her sob again, deeply.

He feeds them cabbage soup and black bread. When he passes a jug of vodka to Elazar, Raḥel drinks from it as well, feeling it burn down her throat, warm her limbs.

Have you seen partisans, Elazar asks the farmer. Or

other Jews, hiding in the forest?

A group of fighters came through here two days ago. I gave them what food I could, one of my shotguns. Raḥel, your mother . . .?

He sees the look on her face and reflects it in his own, his fury so accentuated by the thick black eyebrows which seem to squirm like caterpillars in the flickering candlelight that Raḥel has to hold in the hysterical laughter that bubbles up from her chest, pushes against her tightened lips. She knows if she lets it out, it will not stop, that it will grow into a wail that all the dead will howl through her mouth. Instead it sprouts as tears which Tcharnetzki awkwardly rubs from her cheek with his large calloused thumb.

A black year on them, he mutters. You will sleep here tonight. Tomorrow I will help you find the forest Jews.

The forest Jews, she thinks. How folkloric. She and Elazar would transform into characters in a fairy tale. Their child, still unnamed, would survive as an elf.

Thank you, Elazar says.

Nonsense.

No. If the Germans find us in your house . . .

You can stay in the barn.

They will do the same if they find us there.

Raḥel lays her hand on the warmth of the farmer's

broad shoulder. For a second, it anchors her. To this kind man, to the soil on which he stood.

We will sleep in the forest, come back in the morning if it is all clear, she lies to him. You have fed us, it is enough, she says, and that is not a lie: the sustenance he's given them is more than food.

Tcharnetzki is silent for a moment, standing with his eyes closed, his shoulders swaying: an argument he is having with himself. He stops, nods, goes to the counter and wraps the rest of the black bread in a cheesecloth.

Take this. I'm sorry, I have no more cheese.

We can't take your last bread, Elazar says.

You better take this as well, Tcharnetzki says, handing him a large carving knife. This time her husband doesn't object.

They move into the tree line, far enough so that the sunrise would not reveal them, gather and pile enough pine needles to keep them off the forest floor. They lie down on the scratchy needles, looking at the stars between the tops of the

trees.

We will not go back to him, Elazar says.

No.

Sleep, rest for an hour or two.

And then where?

He reaches over and lays his hand on her belly. Mars. America. The moon.

· She waves at the trees, the forest.

The Piska, she says.

Yes, he says. The Piska.

The path they follow is dimly lit in moonlight that, when she looks up, becomes sparkling silver coins as it breaks through the leaf canopy. Elazar, in front of her, appears in and out of the shadows like an apparition. Their task, she realizes, is hopeless; that is, it is based only on hope. And desperation. The partisans, if they exist, if they ever existed, could be anywhere. The Piska, America, the moon.

Are you alright, Elazar asks.

Daydreaming, she says.

Stay awake, my love.

At some point they walk near the road that runs from Kolno to Zabiele, staying behind the curtain of trees fringing it. They freeze when they hear the rumble of a vehicle, see light from the headlights of a large lorry illuminating the strip of concrete. Its bed is packed with people, pressed tightly together; closer she can see that they are all women and girls. All Jews.

By sunrise, exhausted, they sit at the base of a huge pin oak and eat a little more of the bread and cheese. She sees Elazar touch the scar on his nose, a gesture so familiar that it brings her back to their home, brings a welling of grief at its loss. He touches his groin and his leg, gestures which she had only become acquainted with in the last months; his condition crowded out of her mind by the events of these last days.

Is it painful?

He moves his hand away quickly, as if she has caught him doing something shameful.

It is nothing.

She waved at the branches arched over their heads. At least it's summer, she says. Once, when my brother was injured, my father dragged him on a sled through this forest during the dead of winter, to a doctor he knew. A German, she added.

Yes. An educated people.

We could have gotten away. We could have gone to America, as my papa wanted me to.

I'm sorry, her husband says.

She could bite her tongue. It had no bones. Even

here, even now, it spoke her mother's bitter words. She wants to swallow them, but they are already out in the world.

You're right; you could have gone with your brothers and sisters to America. I wrenched you from who you were, who you could have been, because I needed you. You were so young. Too young.

Did he think she had no agency? She presses down the anger and sorrow swelling in her heart. Anger and sorrow and, to her surprise, laughter. To hear such mundane lamentations here, now, after all they have seen, all that still awaits them, all they had lost. It referred to a normality that was as distant and abstract as the Afterlife.

What an insulting thing to say. Do you think you pulled me unwilling onto that horse? Cossack, she added. They grin at each other.

He touches his leg. Now this is your burden. This is the *heshboon,* the bill.

A thought comes into her mind; she spits it out before it can nest there. Do you believe Rivka Mendl cursed you?

He laughs. She didn't give me cancer. Nor did the Russians and the Germans come to avenge my insult to her.

She is startled that he has finally named the disease. She has felt; she knows they both have felt, that the last weeks had somehow negated the sickness, as if it were self-indulgent to admit to its progress. She feels a thickening of grief again, in her throat, in her very womb. It is absurd. She knows they will probably die anyway. Why does she have to suffer this as well, to know that wherever they ran an executioner ran with them, dwelt under her husband's skin?

In the market square, at the cemetery, I tried to think of the Germans as dybbuks. To explain them.

They were not dybbuks. They were Germans.

I know.

A sudden mad staccato of drum beats assails their ears. It goes on and on. The trees around them seem to shiver, their leaves tremble. She remembers the lorry, filled with women and children, moving in the direction of Zabiele. Of Zabiele where she had helped dig anti-tank trenches.

She looks at her husband. The sun is almost fully risen now and his face is dappled with the light coming through the leaves woven above them.

What if we'd gotten to Bremen, she asks; what if we'd taken a ship west instead of a train east, saw the Statue, the gleaming towers of the tall buildings waiting for us? That's all I meant.

Her husband smiles.

Raḥel tries to imagine the golden streets and soaring

towers of America, their spires piercing the clouds. But images from the market square and the cemetery, the whipped, the murdered, the raped, and her friend Halima's troubled eyes and Tcharnetzki's beautiful ugly face crowds that dream from her mind's eye. The curses of the past, the paths that could have been taken—such stories have been negated, made ridiculous, rendered as unimportant as the cancer eating her husband's leg. There is no time for regret now, only for love.

She touches her stomach. Elazar, she says. We have never decided on what his name will be.

I'd like to leave them there. Give them infinite possibilities, a thousand paths to take through the woods. Run, I want to tell them. Look at them, those two, under those brooding trees, laced with shadows and sunlight. Look at them, called into the world by the words that have alighted, rallied breath and flesh to their forms. They are in the country of words, they can be cursive, printed, twisted, straightened, written right to left, left to write, horizontal or vertical; anything can happen.

A man named Bocka Eidenberg and a woman named Chaya-Leah Olech had run away from the Kolno market square and taken refuge in a barn. When the farmer found them sleeping in his hay in the morning, he got a German policeman, who arrested the two, put them into a cart and started to take them, with the farmer's help, to the police station. Along the way, somehow Eidenberg got his hands loose: he grabbed the policeman and while he was choking him, Chaya-Leah drew out the man's dagger and stabbed him to death. The farmer managed to run away. The couple, hunted, a price on their heads, hid in the forest until 1944, when the Germans found and killed them.

— The Kolno Memorial Book

I want at least that for them, Raḥel and Elazar, fighters, I want them to have that moment of dignity. But how could I take it away from Eidenberg and Olech, those brave, desperate souls?

Run, I want to shout at them. They can go anywhere. They can be betrayed, caught, tossed into a cart, and yes, Elazar the *boevik* getting his hands around their betrayer's neck, Raḥel the fighter stabbing him, and they will disappear into the forest, find the Jewish partisans, as their cousins Avrahmam, Dov, and Yitzhak Lobel did, fight valiantly, survive the war, immigrate, live for years before the cancer he refuses to see as a curse from the woman he abandoned creeps up my father's leg.

Or they can disappear down another path, find a witch, magic dwarves that bring them to crystal caverns.

Or Argamaka, resurrected, can come galloping out of the trees and once again they leap up onto her broad back and ride away.

But there is an obscenity about imagining from need. About fluidity. Didn't the Poles and the Germans imagine the Jews they needed, configured them from hate and longing and envy into forms so false and yet so true to their creators' nature that all they longed to do was bury them?

I am one of those who were not there during the 'Black Days' when those nearest and dearest to us were hurled into a common grave dug by their own hands," wrote Herschel Kolinsky. *"I did not hear their prayers at the brink of the grave, but only years later—from afar—did I hear their echoes. We, who were not there, still cannot believe that the things we heard about had really taken place."*

— The Kolno Memorial Book

I know what has to occur, and this is not a folk tale nor a fairy tale; this is about what happened and what didn't happen and what will keep happening. It is about loss that must be held up into the light to find how it can speak to love.

Chapter Twenty-Four: The Ditch

They are separated for the last time when they reach the market square and are thrown from the cart onto the cobblestones, their hands still bound. Raḥel tries to twist her face as she falls, to avoid a direct blow from the stones, but they strike her right forehead hard. Blood runs down into her eyes. Through the red mist she sees her husband rising, struggling towards her, roaring. A soldier kicks out his ankles and he falls. Two other soldiers bend and take him under his arms, and drag him to the other side of the square where the truck awaits, already filled with men. The Jewish men of Kolno. She wills her insides to fill with cold iron. Feels it make a wall behind her eyes. It tastes like iodine. It encases her heart, the walls of her womb. She will not cry. She will not feel. To feel, one must have hope. She looks to see her husband one last time as the truck pulls away.

Goodbye, my love.

"On the 15th of July," a man named Koncepolsky-Chludniewitz remembered, *"the Germans commanded all*

the men, aged sixteen and above, to gather in the market square and bring food for one day with them, as they would be going out to work." When they arrived, the men were loaded into and then driven away in four lorries to the defensive trenches many of them must have helped dig. They were never seen again, though "After some days the Poles were heard to say that the ground in the trenches . . . had been seen shaking and trembling." Three days later the parents and wives and children of the murdered men were told to report to the market square with luggage and valuables.

They were loaded onto the same trucks and driven to the nearby village of Meschtshevoye, near Stavisk, where they were machine-gunned into a mass grave. The third action took place at the end of July when all the remaining Jews were ordered to the market square. From the descriptions, what happened must have been a combination of a Polish pogrom and the more orderly murder the Germans preferred. The Polish mob, eager to prove itself to the Germans, attacked the Jews gathered there. Babies were torn from their mother's arms and their brains dashed out on the stones: people who tried to run away or to resist and were shot on the spot. The women and children were taken by lorry to Meschtshevoye and machine gunned. The men were made to walk to Kolimagi and machine gunned into ditches there. — The Kolno Memorial Book

In Raḥel's womb, in the ditch, the fetus has come to remember the Concept of Warmth. He can see nothing with his eyes—he has not yet remembered Sight, but now, floating, warm, the growing cells of his skin humming, he feels touched all over, hugged by warmth, as if the flesh around him he has become used to, his mother's flesh, is now being encased by the naked warmth of other women, other mothers and grandmothers and sisters and daughters, all the Jewish women of Kolno, pressed themselves by the walls of the ditch. He feels the embracing weight of them through his mother's flesh, cradling him.

All around him is a dull rumbling. He hears a staccato drumming, muffled by the walls of the womb. The amniotic fluid in which he floats trembles and vibrates.

A jumble of Letters forms behind his eyes. Lines and curves and points. They are windows. He peers into each one. Whatever he sees is instantly named to him. He does not hear the names. They settle on him like a cloud of butterflies, whisper in his ears, trace their forms on his skin. He absorbs them and they flow into his blood and swell in his brain and understanding and become Light. A man and a woman, smile down at him, seen through wooden bars of a crib. Their laughter dances him into the air. He glides onto a street where tall buildings gleaming with windows canyon around him and flashing lights dance before his eyes and cars, honking like geese, bear down on him and concrete streets transform into endless roads and then into horned water buffalo wading ponderously in an emerald patchwork of flooded rice fields that mirror the sun and he is flying above the rice fields that move like carpets beneath him and in their reflection he is a dragon fly, hanging like a moving, threatening shadow over the fields and then over a village of thatched roofs and then over a ditch. As they sink lower, he sees green men on the edge of the ditch and people packed in it, lying as close together as fetuses in a womb, as close as the women around him in a ditch in Poland. He is in both places at once and above them also and he sees the ditch extending and branching north and south and east and west pushing like a forming river over years and miles and lands, filled with the dead and the soon to be dead, until the face of the earth is crisscrossed with a cicatrix of ditches and a Voice tells him to go in among the dead and see if there is one ready to be born. So he wades into the ditch, tripping, falling into the corpses, his legs continually caught and held as they slip between arms and armpits, or between legs, or sink into the softness of throats, into the entangled stories of all these lives embraced together now; they catch and hold him and release him until he hears the cry of a living child. And he draws that child out of the embrace of the dead as out of a womb and as he cradles it in his arms, weeping, he writes Letters on my forehead with his trembling finger. I feel the letters, Aleph, Vav, Rash, Mem, אברם form and settle on my skin as he moves into me and becomes me, and as I absorb them they line up into my name. Avram. And as my name claims me, cradling me in the arms of its letters, I remember the World and its joys and griefs and I see the letters of my name are now doors, each letter a door, and one of them opens to a room near the sea where a black-haired woman smiles at me as all around us again our stories are nestling and whispering and waiting again to be born.

Author's Note

In 1996 I published a book called *Rumors and Stones,* a non-fiction account of a journey I made in 1993 to Poland that includes an attempt to describe my parents'—though mostly my mother's—life in the town of Kolno, and how she and our family immigrated to the United States. The book also recounts what happened to those Jews, including unnamed family members, who stayed in Poland and later were murdered, along with over 2,000 other Kolno Jews. I made the journey after my mother's death, in 1991, and just before a trip I took to Vietnam, my first time back in that country since I had been a Marine there in the Vietnam war. Both of those journeys from a peaceful present that sat uneasily on a violent past fused in my mind and in the way I ended up writing about them.

Besides the non-fiction reportage in the book, the "Stones," I attempted to make my mother's life in Kolno more immediate and personal to readers, and to myself, by recalling the stories about that life she had told me and re-imagining them, putting myself into her consciousness or into the consciousness of her parents or siblings. These became the "Rumors" in the book. Writing from my mother's imagined point of view, even as, or perhaps especially as, a created character, had been one way I dealt with her loss.

Last year, the press which carries *Rumors and Stones* decided to put out a digital edition of the book. When I went to provide the digital files, I found that several of the Rumors chapters were missing, and I had to re-type them into my computer. As I did, I recalled how when I first wrote the book, I had debated whether those imagined scenes should be published separately as fiction, or be developed into a longer narrative, as a novel or novella.

But for the most part, except for editing some work I'd already finished, I had stopped writing. In 2020, I suffered the loss of my wife of over forty years, and the promises of art, to illuminate, to give hope and purpose, to exert control had become hollow, mocking. I no longer knew to whom I was writing, or indeed if I still believed the truth articulated by Tim O'Brien that "stories save lives." It was a feeling inextricable from my personal loss, and reinforced by the perception that the stuggles of the last fifty years since the war had been futile, that the arc of history had not in fact moved towards justice, that my country and the world seemed to be regressing into lies and violence, trembling to pieces in ways that brought back all the losses of the war as if they had occurred now instead of half a century ago.

Then last year, I looked at a story I had written previously, "The Genizah" and discovered what I hadn't seen in it previously: how much of it was about loss and grief and the attempt of art to shape grace and meaning and control out of what Ferlinghetti called "the empty air of existence." I re-wrote the story, hewing it, as the sculptor Rae does within it, to what I now saw was its true shape. Its last lines and images led my mind back to the fiction in *Rumors and Stones,* my mother's so-human tales of hardship, love, strength and defeat and triumph; how a tough family had pulled themselves out of a straitjacket of fear and oppression and came to this country, drawn to its promise while always remaining aware of its imperfections, fueled by the same iron determination to define their lives rather than have them defined by others that I saw in my wife, herself an immigrant. Looking at that story, I thought it would be a fitting way to include, continue, and add to the stories in *Rumors and Stones*, to speak to the ways in which stories can save lives. But the stories, the way I'd tried to know and connect to those lives through them, led me to another question. I had always felt a profound gratitude that my family had left Poland and came to America. It was one of the reasons I had attempted to serve my country in what turned out to be a bad war. I knew what their fate would have been. In *Rumors and Stones,* I had also recounted what had happened to those Jews who remained in Kolno, until the Germans came and that community ended forever. Through information from the internet that was not available in the 1990s when I wrote the book, I also found the names I had not known before: twenty-three victims carrying our family name, the Brikmans of Kolno, and thirty-five from the extended Lobel family of Kolno and Jedwabne—Sarah Gittel's family—were among the murdered, including her brother Tzvi Haim Lobel, his wife Miriam Beili, and her other brother, Avraham Yitzhak Lobel, after whom I was named; his wife Gittel Tovah and their children Zelda, Rivka, Shalom, and Pinchas.

That word, murdered, in its unadorned accuracy, is repeated over and over in the list of the dead from Kolno in the Shoah Database of Holocaust Victims from Yad VaShem. I also found the stories I didn't know of those who had escaped: Avraham and Gittel's daughter Bruria Lobel to Palestine, her brothers Haim, Moshe, and Zelig to Argentina, and Tzvi and Miriam's sons Dov, Yitzhak, and Avraham Lobel, who fled to the forest and joined the partisans, fought with the Russian army into Berlin, were among the liberators of Auschwitz and ended up living on a kibbutz in Israel.

Weaving the “rumors” stories that tried to imagine my parents’ lives through incidents about which my mother had told me into a narrative that imagined what could have happened if my immediate family did not leave, did not find the refuge of America, is—I hope—a way I can commemorate and mourn the real victims by bringing what happened to them into my own life and mourning, by making it present, in the spirit of the Passover Seder which admonishes those at the table to recount the liberation from slavery in Egypt as if it had happened to themselves.

It is, I also hope, a way to speak, to plead “stop” to all the hopeless cycles of murder that will always occur when we refuse to exercise the ability of our imaginations to inhabit the minds and lives of those on the other side of the Pale, the fence, the borders between us.

May the memory of the victims be for a blessing.

May my mother Rhoda Karlin’s, ne Raḥel Brickman, memory be for a blessing.

May my father Louis Karlin’s, ne Elazar Karlinsky, memory be for a blessing.

May my wife, Ohnmar Thein Karlin’s, ne Ohnmar Thein, memory be for a blessing.

Acknowledgments

With gratitude for my early readers, Michael Glaser, George Evans, and Nguyễn Phan Quế Mai, for their encouragement and suggestions; to Avishai Bashan and Yaara Bashan Haham for their help finding and gathering family information, and to my publisher Caleb Mason, for his vision and faith in this book.

Other Books by Wayne Karlin

Fiction:

Crossover
Lost Armies
The Extras
Us
Prisoners
The Wished for Country
Marble Mountain
A Wolf by the Ears
Memorial Days: Việt Nam Stories, 1973-2022

Non-Fiction:

Rumors and Stones: A Journey
War Movies: Scenes and Outtakes
Wandering Souls: Journeys with the Dead and the Living in Việt Nam

As Co-Editor:

Free Fire Zone: Short Stories by Vietnam Veterans, with Basil T. Paquet and Larry Rottmann
The Other Side of Heaven: Postwar Fiction by Vietnamese and American Writers, with Lê Minh Khuê and Trường Vũ
Love After War: Contemporary Fiction from Vietnam. with Hồ Anh Thái

Appendix

Below are the murdered family members taken from *The Central Database of Shoah Victims' Names,* sorted by family name and place of residence:

The Central Database of Shoah Victims' Names

✖ Last / Maiden Name = Brikman ✖ Place = Kolno, Poland

24 results for Victims/individuals
24 results for Records/documents

Page 1 of 1

Last Name	First Name	Birth ...	Place of Residence	Fate
Brikman	Chaim Pinkas Leibel		Kolno, Poland	murdered
Brikman	Avraham		Kolno, Poland	murdered
Brikman	Getzol		Kolno, Poland	murdered
Brikman	Hershel		Kolno, Poland	murdered
Brikman	Breina		Kolno, Poland	murdered
Brikman	Zerakh		Kolno, Poland	murdered
Brikman	Bashka		Kolno, Poland	murdered
Brikman	Sara Feigel		Kolno, Poland	murdered
Brikman	Rivka		Kolno, Poland	murdered

Page 1 of 1

Page 1 of 1

Last Name	First Name	Birth ...	Place of Residence	Fate
Brikman	Yaakov		Kolno, Poland	murdered
Brikman	Gitel		Kolno, Poland	murdered
Brikman	Faivel		Kolno, Poland	murdered
Brikman	Meichli		Kolno, Poland	murdered
Brikman	Sheina Ester		Kolno, Poland	murdered
Brikman	Liba		Kolno, Poland	murdered
Brikman	Neshka		Kolno, Poland	murdered
Brikman	Reizl		Kolno, Poland	murdered
Brykman	Sara		Kolno, Poland	murdered
Brykman	Chaim Mendel		Kolno, Poland	murdered
Brykman	Matul Motel		Kolno, Poland	murdered
Brykman	Shalom		Kolno, Poland	murdered
Brykman	Tuvia		Kolno, Poland	murdered
Shober	Sara		Kolno, Poland	murdered
Shober Shever	Rivka Rachel		Kolno, Poland	murdered

Page 1 of 1

The Central Database of Shoah Victims' Names

✖ Last / Maiden Name = Lobel ✖ Place = Kolno, Poland

37 results for Victims/individuals

37 results for Records/documents

Page 1 of 1

Last Name	First Name	Birth ...	Place of Residence	Fate
Kac	Lea	1902	Kolno, Poland	murdered
Lobel	Avraham Velvel		Kolno, Poland	murdered
Lobel	Itka		Kolno, Poland	murdered
Lobel	Bezhi		Kolno, Poland	murdered
Lobel	Beila		Kolno, Poland	murdered
Lobel	Braintzi		Kolno, Poland	murdered
Lobel	Zusman		Kolno, Poland	murdered
Lobel	Fist Name Unknown		Kolno, Poland	murdered
Lobel	Berl		Kolno, Poland	murdered
Lobel	Asna		Kolno, Poland	murdered
Lobel	Shmuelik		Kolno, Poland	murdered
Lobel	Sheina		Kolno, Poland	murdered
Lobel	Yehudit		Kolno, Poland	murdered
Lobel	Golda		Kolno, Poland	murdered
Lobel	Toibe		Kolno, Poland	murdered

Page 1 of 1

Page 1 of 1

Last Name	First Name	Birth ...	Place of Residence	Fate
Lobel	Yehoshua		Kolno, Poland	murdered
Lobel	Yaakov		Kolno, Poland	murdered
Lobel	Henia Khava		Kolno, Poland	murdered
Lobel	Sara		Kolno, Poland	murdered
Lobel	Sheina Gitel		Kolno, Poland	murdered
Lobel	Avraham		Kolno, Poland	murdered
Lobel	Yitzhak Mordekhai		Kolno, Poland	murdered
Lobel	Leibel		Kolno, Poland	murdered
Lobel	Golda		Kolno, Poland	murdered
Lobel	Raicha		Kolno, Poland	murdered
Lobel	Nekhama		Kolno, Poland	murdered
Lobel	Ester		Kolno, Poland	murdered
Lobel	Nakhum		Kolno, Poland	murdered
Lobel	Dina		Kolno, Poland	murdered
Lobel	Tzvi		Kolno, Poland	murdered
Lobel	Miriam Beila		Kolno, Poland	murdered
Lobel	Shmuel		Kolno, Poland	murdered
Lobel	Sara		Kolno, Poland	murdered
Lobel	Mindl		Kolno, Poland	murdered
Lobel	Ester		Kolno, Poland	murdered
Löbel Libel	Arie	1917	Kolno, Poland	murdered
Panich	Sara		Kolno, Poland	murdered

Page 1 of 1

The Central Database of Shoah Victims' Names

✖ Last / Maiden Name = Lubel ✖ Place = Jedwabne, Poland

11 results for Victims/individuals

11 results for Records/documents

Page 1 of 1

Last Name	First Name	Birth ...	Place of Residence	Fate
Lubel	Avraham Yitzkhak		Jedwabne, Poland	murdered
Lubel	Gitel		Jedwabne, Poland	murdered
Lubel	Yitzkhak		Jedwabne, Poland	murdered
Lubel	Abraham Jchak	1891	Jedwabne, Poland	murdered
Lubel	Pinchas	1927	Jedwabne, Poland	murdered
Lubel Loevel	Sahra		Jedwabne, Poland	murdered
Lubel Loevel	Jakob Josef		Jedwabne, Poland	murdered
Lubel Loevel	Gitla	1889	Jedwabne, Poland	murdered
Lubel Loevel	Shalom	1925	Jedwabne, Poland	murdered
Lubel Loevel	Pinches	1928	Yedwabne, Poland	murdered
Lubel Loevel	Rivka	1925	Yedwabne, Poland	murdered

Page 1 of 1